THE
HIDDEN
LIGHT

THE HIDDEN LIGHT

A LIFE OF SAINT DOMINIC

JENNIFER MOORCROFT

authorHOUSE®

AuthorHouse™ UK Ltd.
1663 Liberty Drive
Bloomington, IN 47403 USA
www.authorhouse.co.uk
Phone: 0800.197.4150

Published by AuthorHouse   10/29/2013

ISBN: 978-1-4918-8129-3 (sc)
ISBN: 978-1-4918-8130-9 (e)

Library of Congress Control Number: 2013918200

CONTENTS

—

INTRODUCTION

Saint Dominic has been described by one of his biographers, Guy Bedouelle OP,[1] as 'hidden in the light'. Unlike most other founders of religious orders, he says, we have only three brief letters and almost none of his words preserved.; 'we know nothing of Dominic's life except what we can see through the eyes of his followers or his friends . . . The fact that our access to St. Dominic is so indirect reveals his discretion and, in a sense, his detachment from himself. This detachment in turn is an eloquent statement of the place he wished to hold within the Church.'

For the title of this book I have reversed that description somewhat to call Dominic 'the hidden light', because developments at this time have, in a sense, further hidden his light from our view. In the words of Michael Baigent, Dominic was 'a cruel and fanatical Spanish monk'[2] because of his association with the Spanish Inquisition and his persecution of the Cathars. Now the Catholic Church is not in the habit of canonising the cruel and fanatical, but only those who have exhibited heroic

---

[1] *Saint Dominic, The Grace of the Word*, Ignatius Press 1995 p.49

[2] *The Jesus Papers*, Michael Baigent P 95, Harper Element 2006

love of God and neighbour. Could Baigent's description possibly be true?

I knew hardly anything of Dominic before I started writing this book, apart from that possible connection with the infamous Spanish Inquisition, and also the brief meeting he had with St. Francis of Assisi, in which the colourful personality of Francis rather overshadowed that of Dominic.

By contrast with that description of Dominic as cruel and fanatical, Lacordaire described Dominic thus:

> Scarcely one ray falls on Dominic's cappa, yet
> so pure and holy is he that this little light is
> in itself a brilliant witness. The light is hidden
> because the man of God is far from the noise
> and blood of the battle; because, faithful to his
> mission, he opens his mouth only to bless, his
> heart to pray, and his hand to work for love;
> and because virtue, when it stands alone, is lit
> only by the light of God.[3]

These are the two conflicting descriptions of Dominic that I had before me as I set off on a journey to discover the real Dominic. There were other things I wanted to find out, too, because in many ways the challenges that Dominic faced in his day are very similar to those that Catholics face today. Since the discovery of the Gnostic writings at Nag Hammadi there has been an upsurge in interest in Gnosticism and its medieval development in Catharism. I wanted to find out how Dominic actually met the challenge of Catharism, and how we as Catholics can respond to the belief that the Gnostic writings are the

---

[3]   Quoted in Bedouelle p.59

true 'gospel' in contrast to the Catholic proclamation of the Gospel.

Dominic's Order of Preachers was founded at a time when the great universities of the western world were being founded, and his own Order attracted two of the greatest intellects, not only of his time, but of all time, St. Albert the Great and St. Thomas Aquinas. One of the challenges we face today is the conflict between faith and reason, and faith and science, that is one of the concerns of Pope Benedict XV1. Can we learn anything from them as to how to marry faith and reason today?

Then, both Pope John Paul 11 and Pope Benedict XV1 have identified relativism as one of the greatest challenges of our time; that is, the assertion that there is no ultimate truth and that therefore all 'truths' are equal in value—apart, of course, apart from religious belief which is seen by some as being completely worthless. Dominic had the temerity to give his order as its motto, the single word 'Veritas', Truth. So can we still say that there is objective truth, and how would Dominic reply?

One last thing: there are many accounts of miraculous happenings in Dominic's life. Are these to be seen as pious embellishments, or did they really happen? It must be up to each reader to make the judgment for himself. But the accounts of the miraculous events were recorded by the people who knew Dominic and lived with him, and who recorded the other events of his life, too. It may be wise not to dismiss them too easily. But even if they did not happen, they do tell something of the reverence in which he was held, and his closeness to God that instigated such embellishments; the miraculous does happen sometimes around those close to God, and also around those whom

God calls to carry out some special mission in the life of the Church.

I was for some time fortunate in belonging to a parish that for many years has been served by Dominican sisters based in Bushey, England. I have seen in the lives of Sister Anthony and Sister Clare, of Sister Alphonsus and Sister Loretta, the charism of the Order of Preachers being lived out today. I want to dedicate this book to them, and with gratitude to the Bushey community who kindly lent me material to help me in my researches.

CHAPTER 1

EARLY LIFE

Legend recounts that the noble lady, Joanna of Aza, had a dream before the birth of her third son. In it she dreamt she was carrying, instead of a baby, a dog or hound that, when born, bounded away from her with a lighted torch in its mouth that would set the world on fire. It was a prophetic dream, or perhaps a later, evocative understanding, of his name, Dominic, Domini canem, the hound of God, and accurately reflected his God-given calling. Like his Master, the Hound of Heaven, Dominic would be on fire with the love of souls that he would pursue, by his prayers, his sacrifices, his love and his zeal, down the highways and byways of the world.

Birth

Dominic was born in the little village of Caleruega, some twenty miles from the city of Osma in Old Castile, Spain about the year 1170. It was a small and dusty village, but possessed of a special quality of light and clarity in the air, a fitting birthplace, then, of one who always sought the clarity and light of truth. At his baptism his mother witnessed another marvel, a bright star resting on his forehead. This, too, was prophetic, because those who knew him testify to the radiance of his face and its expressiveness.

He was the third son, with Antonio the eldest, followed by Manes and was named Dominic after Saint Dominic of Silo, the patron saint of expectant mothers, with a Benedictine abbey dedicated to him a few miles from Caleruega.

Saintly Parents

His father, Felix Guzman was, like his mother, of noble birth, but it was far more the nobility of their characters that shaped Dominic's early life. Felix was esteemed by the whole village for his Christian devotion. He probably died young, for not much is known about him. From their mother, Joanna, all three boys learnt compassion, respect and concern for the poor, to whom their house and their purse were always open. It is related that, one day when her husband was away on business, Joanna, having nothing else to give to poor and needy villagers, gave away a large jar of wine. On her husband's return, some of the villagers secretly told him what she had done, and when he reached home he asked for wine. Joanna went to the cellar and knelt before the empty jar and prayed. She had already discerned the exceptional holiness of her youngest son, and so asked the Lord, through his merits, to work a miracle. He did so; rising and examining the jar, Joanna found the jar full of wine, which served not only her husband but the whole household. Such was her holiness that she was beatified by Pope Leo X11. Of her other two sons, Antonio became a secular priest, and as the heir to the Guzman wealth, distributed it to the poor and spent his life ministering to the sick in a hospice near the village. Mannes would follow Dominic into the Order his brother founded, and was beatified by Gregory XV1. Such were the fruits of the example of holy living their parents gave them.

Schooling

It was the custom between upper-class Spanish households of the day to send their boys, when they reached seven years of age, either to a baron, if they were destined for a secular career, or to a cleric, if destined for a career in the Church. Both his elder brothers had been sent away to clerics for their education, and with Dominic's evident desire for a career in the Church, even at that early age, his parents made a further sacrifice and he was sent to his mother's brother, a priest, living at Gumiel de Izán, a small town twenty miles away.

It was a wise choice. His uncle proved to be an excellent tutor and guide to a boy of exceptional intelligence, and Dominic thrived in an atmosphere of peace, study and prayer. He learned to read and write, mastering the rules of grammar, and found he delighted in music. He was taught Latin, vital for his future as a priest, a calling that drew him more and more. He loved the liturgy and the psalms, learning many of them off by heart. Under his uncle's guidance he served at Mass and immersed himself in all the spiritual riches of the Church. He proved to be an ardent student, loving to learn and to expand his mind with all the general knowledge his uncle could supply.

Awaking to the World

Gumiel de Izán might have been a small town, and the priest's rectory a haven of peace and study, but it was on the pilgrim way to Compostella and the world streamed past its door. Pilgrims would stop on their way and regale the avid child with stories of faraway places. They told of the struggle to repulse the Moors from Spain; pilgrims from Italy would speak of the pagan Tartar hordes infiltrating from the north, savage men who knew nothing of Jesus Christ. Any child would be both frightened and fascinated by these stories told round the fireside, but for Dominic this natural fascination with these exotic tales would have had the added Christian sensibility that awoke him to the realisation of souls to be won, and a vast mission field awaiting him far from his small town.

Dominic spent seven years with his uncle until he was more than ready to progress to the renowned Cathedral school at Palencia, one of the best seats of learning in Spain at the time. It was to achieve a short-lived status as a university in 1212, providing the model for the University of Salamanca, which was to overshadow it and lead to its demise later that century. He spent ten years there.

University

The first three years were spent studying the Arts, which included Grammar, Logic and Philosophy. Dominic took part in disputations and discussions which trained his mind to think logically and to express his thoughts clearly. It trained him in the arts of the orator, all of which would stand him in good stead later. The next three years were given over to what was called the 'exact sciences', covering Arithmetic, Geometry, Music and Astronomy. The Arts, which nourished the aesthetic senses, were thus balanced by the rigour of Mathematics, giving the medieval mind that rounded, cultured and balanced education which could then progress to the 'Queen of Sciences', Sacred Scripture and Theology.

Studies

Dominic's favourite study was that of Scripture, the basis of all theology. He loved, especially, the Gospel of Saint Matthew and the Epistles of Saint Paul; he learnt them by heart, and kept copies of them next to his heart on his later travels. But he not only studied the Scriptures, he prayed them. All his studies were directed to the service of God, and deepened and enriched by an ever closer union with Him, through nights spent in prayer.

His Charity

Dominic could have become so bookish that he lost sight of the world around him, but the social conscience he had inherited from his parents prevented that. Palencia, despite its relative wealth, was not immune from the famines that often devastated the countryside around, and towards the end of his stay there a famine of unusual intensity ravaged the area. The poor were dying of starvation. Dominic sold off all his possessions, clothing and furniture, and gave away all the money he had, to pay for food for them, until he had only his precious books left. These were indispensable to him as a student; as well, this was before the era of the printing press, every costly volume had to be written by hand on parchment made from sheep skin, and Dominic had annotated his books with his indispensable notes. He did not hesitate; these, too, he sold for food for the starving people. When questioned as why he had made such a heroic gesture he replied, 'I do not wish to study these dead skins while people are dying of hunger'.

Such heroism did not go unnoticed, and others were encouraged to pool their resources to help everyone recover from the effects of the famine. For Dominic, study and books were not an end in themselves, but the indispensable means by which he could nourish his own relationship with God and then feed the souls of others for their salvation. He was later to remark that he learned more from the book of Charity than from any other text because, he said, 'it teaches everything'.

Another example of that charity and concern for others was when he even offered to sell himself into slavery when a woman came to him in tears because her brother had been taken captive by the Moors. The offer was not accepted.

A contemporary, Brother Ventura, testified that 'No one ever talked to Dominic without feeling better for it.' and another near contemporary, Theodoric of Alpoldia, said that he never wasted time and always seemed to be in a hurry—but without sacrificing his availability to those who needed him.

The university masters and students were not the only ones to have taken note of Dominic's exceptional qualities, and as his studies came to an end he received an invitation that he could not resist.

CHAPTER 2

THE HIDDEN YEARS

Dominic lived in a time of ferment. The Moorish advance across Europe had been pushed back—even Dominic's home town of Caraluega had seen the struggle against the Moorish invasion. The situation had eased there, but there were further challenges to face. Nations were coalescing and the population expanding at an unprecedented rate. Small rural communities were changing in nature—and the social cohesion they represented—as towns sprang up and grew larger, encouraging migration into the urban areas in search of work which often was not there, giving rise to an increase in destitution. Above all, heresies and popular movements hostile to the Church were growing in strength and importance.

All this proved a challenge to the Church and often it was unable to respond as it should. There was a great spiritual hunger that often was not being satisfied by the Church. Many of the clergy were uneducated and ignorant of the faith they were meant to pass on so their people suffered and often went elsewhere to find the spirituality for which they yearned. On the other hand, the Guzman family were surely not unique in the depth of their spiritual life and love for God which they expressed in social concern for the poor, and the uncle was surely not the only wise and holy priest who could inspire a young child like Dominic to follow in his footsteps.

Reforms at Osma

The current Pope, Celestine 111, was acutely aware of the situation and was putting in train measures to rectify the situation. As well as reforming many Church structures the Pope issued instructions to his bishops to instigate reforms in their dioceses. The Bishop of Osma, the holy Don Martin Bazan, had already set reforms in train in his diocese, starting with his own priests and his own chapter, and had marked out the young Dominic Guzman to help him in this. Although the canons of the chapter were not a religious order, Bazan had decreed that they would be known as Canons Regular of Saint Augustine, observing the Rule of Saint Augustine and wearing a white tunic under a rochet, with a black mantle when in choir. The bishop and the Prior of the cathedral chapter, Don Diego d'Acebes, now wanted ardent young men to devote themselves within the cathedral precincts to a life of prayer, devout celebration of the liturgy and instruction of the faithful. They had noted the exceptional quality of the young student, his infectious joy that was coupled with personal asceticism, his kindness and thoughtfulness to those around him and a maturity unusual in one so young. Dominic was invited to join them and he eagerly accepted. As soon as he had completed his studies he was clothed with the black and white of the cathedral canons and soon after was ordained to the priesthood.

A Life of Prayer

The Cathedral routine was the ideal life for Dominic, where he could pursue a life of intense contemplative prayer that was punctuated by the regular liturgical services within the cathedral. He preached, and continued his studies of the Scriptures and theology. He was also Sacristan, a task he loved since it brought him into close contact with all that pertained to the altar.

Although Dominic did not realise it, the years at the cathedral were a form of novitiate for him. He discovered *The Conferences of the Fathers of the Desert* by Abbot John Cassian and this became his guide in the ways of prayer. He spent many of his nights in prayer either on the floor of his cell or on the altar steps,—even as a young child he preferred sleeping on the floor rather than in his bed—and his fellow canons could often hear him weeping and praying aloud. With Dominic's deep and persistent self-effacing humility that concealed as much as he could of his inner life, it is good that we have testimony of those nights spent in prayer. His first biographer, Jordan of Saxony, testified that his prayers, tears and intense intercession were for souls whom he longed to bring to Christ. He prayed also for the gift of true charity for himself. He understood profoundly that unless his apostolic zeal for souls flowed from the love of God Himself, which is the very life of the Trinity, then it would not be fruitful for eternity. So his prayer was two-pronged, for himself and for souls; above all, that he would be brought into ever closer union with Christ, because he realised that he could not preach effectively to others unless he himself lived a life of holiness and total self-sacrifice. The holier he could become, the more the love of God could flow freely through him, the more he could be of benefit for souls. His prayer was not a selfish seeking after holiness for its own sake, but was watered by his intense desire for the salvation of souls, or as an early source put it, that he might open 'the intimate sanctuary of his compassion' to the world.

So esteemed was he by his community that in 1201, at the earliest opportunity, he was elected sub-Prior. Shortly afterwards Bishop Bazan died and Don Diego was appointed Bishop in his stead. Then, in 1203, King Alphonso 111 of Castile commissioned Bishop Diego to go as his ambassador to Denmark to negotiate the marriage between the King's son and a Danish princess. Don Diego chose Dominic to travel with him as his companion.

Mission to Denmark

The entourage passed through the Province of Toulouse in the south of France, and the Bishop and Dominic were made aware, not only of those who had lapsed from the Faith, but of those who had deliberately turned away from the Church to embrace other forms of belief, such as Catharism and its allied branch of Albigensianism. One evening they lodged at an inn and Dominic discovered that the inn-keeper was an Albigensian. He sat up all that night talking with him, but first of all he listened to the inn-keeper's reasons as to why he had left the Church. Carefully and clearly Dominic responded to all his host's objections and problems, explained the Faith to him, and had the joy of reconciling the man to the Church. It was a seminal experience for Dominic, but for the present his first duty was to his Bishop and their mission.

In Denmark they were received warmly and the negotiations went well. Dominic received further fuel for his apostolic zeal as he became aware of vast lands beyond Denmark that had never received the Faith. These were the steppes of Central Asia east of the Caspian Sea and the inhabitants, the Turks and Mongols, were falling to the Muslims.

Second Mission

Their mission completed, the Bishop and the King's retinue returned to Spain, but returned two years later to escort the princess back to Spain. To their dismay, this time the mission received a set-back; the princess had entered a convent and by this had annulled her consent to the marriage. To confirm that this was the case in Canon Law the entourage did not return directly to Spain but went to Rome to consult the Papal court on the matter. But Bishop Diego, and undoubtedly Dominic supported him in this, had other matters to discuss. The two men had been profoundly affected by the state of the Cumans, a pagan nomadic tribe in Germany which had invaded Thuringia and ravaged the country as auxiliaries in King Ottokar 1's army. They had never been evangelised. Here was mission territory indeed. Bishop Diego asked to be relieved of his bishopric, which he felt was beyond his capabilities, and also so that he could join a projected mission to these peoples that the Archbishop of Lund, Andrew Suneson, was organising. The Pope emphatically rejected Diego's request, and they began the journey back to Spain.

They stopped at the famous Cistercian monastery of Citeaux, in Burgundy, and Bishop Diego received the Cistercian habit, although he did not himself become a Cistercian. When they left, Diego took with him two Cistercians to instruct him in their way of life, for he hoped they might come and make a foundation in his diocese. At Montpellier they met more Cistercians, three papal legates who had been sent on a preaching expedition to the region to counteract the Cathars, who had been entrenched there for over fifty years. Since the Church was so concerned about the Cathar advance we need to ask what was there about their beliefs that posed such a threat to the Church?

Catharism

The origins of the Cathars, and its closely related branch, the Albigensians, are disputed, but most believe that the sect originated from the Bogomars from Bulgaria, who brought their mixture of Eastern and Gnostic beliefs with them as they migrated west. However, Catharism had its roots in an even more ancient belief system, Gnosticism.

Gnosticism

From the very beginning of its existence, the Church had to respond to the Gnostic religion that infiltrated her and at times almost overwhelmed her. The origins of Gnosticism predate Christianity, and is difficult to define because, like its modern counterpart, the New Age movement, it had many parts and many pick and mix beliefs.

Saint Paul himself encountered Gnostic influences in Corinth, which was a melting pot of many strange beliefs from all over the Roman world. His letters to the Corinthians respond to some of their objections to his apostolic teaching against the influence Gnosticism had over them. In his first letter to them he picks up on some of their objections, and his response to them lays the ground for the Church's teaching ever since. Gnosticism is a dualist religion, that is, they believed that there was a good god that created the spiritual aspect of man and an evil god that had created the material world. Because some of the Corinthians were arguing that since there was a duality between body and spirit, then it did not matter what they did with their bodies: 'All things are lawful to me'. (1 Corinthians 6:12) Further, because actions done by the body could not affect the soul, 'Food is meant for the stomach and the stomach for food and God will destroy both the one and the other' (v13), then it did not matter what one did with the body because it did not have an eternal destiny. At one extreme one could engage in an asceticism that eschewed marriage, or on the other extreme one could engage in any indulgence of the flesh since it had no influence on the soul.

Not so, was Saint Paul's reply. The body is meant for the Lord, not for immorality, because God will raise both the soul and the body by virtue of the Lord's own resurrection. Our body is a temple of the Holy Spirit, and we have been bought at the price of the death and resurrection of Christ himself. 'So glorify God in your body'. (v 20) This was the importance of his insistence on the Resurrection of Jesus, both of soul and transformed body, because if Christ has not been raised then we have not been raised and there will be no resurrection of the body (cf 1 Cor. 15).

Saint John also had to confront the Gnostic challenge, writing of 'many deceivers have gone out into the world, men who will not acknowledge the coming of Jesus Christ in the flesh' (11 John v7) and responded in a similar manner, stressing the reality of Christ as the Word made flesh: 'Which we have heard, which we have seen with our own eyes, which we have looked upon and touched with our own hands, concerning the Word of Life' (1 John 1:1).

Gnosticism proved a major threat to Christianity in the early centuries, since it took into itself some elements of Christianity. In the process it so distorted the Christian Gospel that although it is fashionable to talk of 'Gnostic Christians' and 'Gnostic Christianity' it is more truthfully anti-Christian Gnosticism, because there is in it hardly a belief that is genuinely Christian. Rather, it is a denial of all that Christianity is while using some Christian terminology, just as the Cathars were to do. A modern Gnostic expressed it in this way:

> Gnosticism is a system of direct experiential knowledge of God, the Soul of the Universe. In the early centuries of this era, among a growing Christianity, it took the form of the Christian faith, while rejecting most of its specific beliefs. Its wording is therefore largely Christian, while its spirit is that of the latest paganism of the West.[4]

Origen, in the 2nd Century, was one of the most influential of the Church Fathers to write extensively in

---

[4]   Duncan Greenlees, quoted in *The books the Church Suppressed*, Michael Green, P. 104

response to it. In just one example, he very concisely puts the Gnostic beliefs and the Christian response to it:

> Not one of the heretics is of the opinion that the Word was made flesh. If you examine their creeds carefully, you will find that, in every one of them, the Word of God is presented as without flesh and incapable of suffering, as is 'the Christ who is above'. Some say that He revealed Himself as a transfigured man, but was not born or made flesh. Others deny that He took human form at all. They say that He descended in the form of a dove, on the Jesus born of Mary . . . and after He had announced the 'unknown Father', He went up again into the 'divine Pleroma' . . . The Lord's disciple shows all these people to be false witnesses when he says, 'And the Word was made flesh and dwelt among us' (John 1:14)[5]

As can be seen from this brief extract. There were variations to Gnostic beliefs, but all of them deny the reality of Christ's being as both true God and true Man.

The Cathar Threat

Although Gnostic beliefs were known for centuries only through the writings of its opponents such as Origen, until the discovery of the Nag Hammadi texts in the early part of the twentieth century, their beliefs persisted like an

---

[5] See *The Scandal of the Incarnation*, Irenaeus Against the Heresies, Hans Urs von Balthasar Ignatius Press 1990 P. 14

underground stream on the fringes of Christianity in such movements as the Manichees, of which Saint Augustine was at one point a follower, and then in the emergence of the Cathars.

The Appeal of Catholicism

That Gnosticism and Catharism have proved so enduring means that it contains elements that have a strong appeal. People have a hunger for a spirituality, of union with the divine and these movements offer an attractive way of fulfilling that hunger. It attracted those who rejected the hierarchical structure of the Church, as are so many of those who are drawn to New Age spirituality and the looser form of evangelical Christianity today. Although Catharism did have its hierarchy, it was not so structured as in the Catholic Church. It was popularly perceived that the Catholic Church and its hierarchy came between the person and God. According to Tobias Churton:

> What was so utterly damnable about the message of the Cathars was that not only was the Church held to be irrelevant in the matter of the soul's redemption but that the Church of Rome was positively the temple of Satan, a false church, a counterfeit produced by the Devil to outwit men and women from true knowledge of themselves and of the work of Christ. The Church had involved itself with political power and worldly vice. Christ had said that a man cannot serve two masters: God and Money. There was among many of the nobles of Languedoc something of a consensus

which held that the Church of Rome was not
the kind of master worth serving [6]

There was also the esoteric element within Gnosticism
and Catharism, the sense that they were superior to the
ordinary Catholic in thrall to their clergy and ignorant of
the higher spirituality to which they were privy.

The Catholic Response

The popularity and widespread acceptance of the Cathars
had long given the Papacy concern as it saw the Catholic
influence wane in face of the hostility and contempt of
the Cathars towards the Church, which in many ways
was understandable, given the woeful state of the Church
in many places. Pope Celestine 111 had died in January
1198, to be succeeded by Pope Innocent 111. The new
Pope, as his predecessors had been, was concerned at the
parlous state of the Church and swiftly initiated reforms
to counteract the Cathar threat. As Pope Innocent wrote
to his legates, 'The pastor has become a hireling; he no
longer feeds the flock, but himself; wolves enter the fold
and he is not there to oppose himself as a wall against the
enemies of God's house.'

The secular authorities, too, were aware of the dangers
to the Church by Cathar beliefs. Although his son,
Raymond V1 of Toulouse, espoused the Cathar cause
when he succeeded to the dukedom, his father, Raymond
V wrote to the abbot of Cîteux of the ravages it was
causing:

---

[6]   *The Gnostics* p.71 Weidenfeld and Nicolson

The putrid scourge of heresy has spread to such a point that most of those who consent to it believe they are thereby giving homage to God . . . the very ones who have given themselves to the priesthood are corrupted by the plague of heresy, and the holy and ever-venerable premises of the churches remain unkempt; they fall into ruin; baptism is denied; the Eucharist is abominated; penance is scorned; the creation of man and the resurrection of the body are rejected, and all the sacraments of the Church are annulled.[7]

Meeting at Montpellier

This excerpt highlights one of the most urgent needs required to counteract the Cathar threat; the priests themselves were so ill-educated and ignorant of their Catholic Faith that they, too, were succumbing to heresy, and taking their flocks with them. It was little wonder, therefore, that the Cistercian mission was having little success in winning back hearts and minds to the Church, and little support from the clergy, either. By the time Bishop Diego and Dominic met them the monks were so depressed that they were ready to abandon their mission.

Pope Innocent was not ready to abandon the mission so easily and had charged twelve more Cistercian abbots to join the three papal legates, plus forty monks of the

---

[7]   As quoted in *Those Terrible Middle Ages*, Regine Pernoud Ignatius Press 2000 P. 122

Order, under the Abbot Arnold of Citeaux. The group were meeting at Montpellier with other bishops and prelates of the surrounding region in council to discuss the situation and what could be done about it. When Bishop Diego—and Dominic—arrived in the city they joined the Cistercians, listening to what was being said and forming their own conclusions, which did not at first meet with everyone's approval.

It was not hard to recognise one of the main reasons for the Cistercians' lack of success. The Cathars, Diego pointed out, lived a simple, even austere life, impressing and winning over others with the holiness of their life, however misguided that outward holiness was. This was in striking contrast, the Bishop said, to the stylish and expensive carriages and furnishings the papal legates used, in keeping with their official status. It was not that the Cistercians lacked simplicity and holiness—Diego and Dominic had been won over by their radical monastic life, but it was not matched by the externals of their apostolate. No wonder the Cathars were able to treat them with contempt for their lack of Gospel simplicity. As one observer remarked, 'Here was a God who always went on foot—yet today his servants ride in comfort. Here was a God of poverty—yet today his missionaries are wealthy. Here was a God humble and scorned of men—yet today his envoys are loaded with honours.' Something obviously had to be done, and the Bishop did it.

'This is not the way, my brothers, this is not the way to go about things,' he urged. 'You cannot win back to the faith by words alone those who are more easily won over by example. If you were to go to them with less poverty and austerity than the Cathars, you will never persuade them. Match steel with steel, the arrogance and false holiness of these false apostles must be overthrown by genuine humility.'

He led by example. With the approval of Pope Innocent 111 for this plan, Diego sent back his horses and provisions and most of his entourage, leaving only a few clergy with him, including Dominic. As for Dominic, he had no need to divest himself of anything, as he loved poverty with a passion, and had nothing to give away. The Cistercians then followed him, going about on foot, begging for their food, taking lodgings where they could find them.

It was in keeping with his character that Bishop Diego would also give the example. He was a man of profound holiness himself, and an outstanding character, full of love and zeal for the faith and the reform of the Church. He also had a deep appreciation of his young sub-prior, recognising leadership qualities in him as well as his holiness, and noting also the profound humility with which he willingly subordinated himself to his Bishop. It was no surprise that there existed between the two men a deep, mutual affection; Dominic found in Diego a true father, and more, a revered father in God, and Diego saw Dominic as a cherished son. So now, as they set out on a mission to the Cathars, Diego could have no better companion.

Debating with the Cathars

They travelled towards Toulouse through Albigensian territory, on foot, in poor clothing, with only their Bibles and a few books, begging for their food. They came to Beziers, where they engaged in debates with the Cathars for fifteen days, strengthening the faith of the few

Catholics there. These debates, and Dominic would have many of them, were formal affairs. A few days beforehand, the protagonists would submit to the secular authorities a complete list of the questions and points of doctrine they wished to raise, and afterwards had to supply the Biblical texts, texts from the theologians and Church Fathers and other authorities they had used in the debates, plus the arguments they used, which were then published in book form. Once an agenda had been agreed, a date was fixed for the opening debate.

What sort of arguments were used in these discussions? Material is very scarce, but Blessed Jordan of Saxony, one of Dominic's first and closest companions, left a partial account of one discussion that took place at Verfeuil in the Carcassonne. The protagonists for the Cathars were Pons Jordan and Arnald Arifat. Starting from the text from John 3:13, 'No one has gone up to heaven except the one who has come down from heaven, the Son of Man,' the Bishop asked the Cathars how they interpreted this text. Dominic, like his bishop, would always try to understand how and why they believed as they did before putting his own arguments, because only in that way could he properly respond to their objections. In reply, the Cathars said that John was speaking of himself, that he was the man in heaven.

'You mean, then,' said the Bishop, 'that his father, who is in heaven, is a man of whom he calls himself the son?'

They replied that this was their understanding. "Then, since the Lord says through Isaiah (66:1) that "Heaven is my throne and the earth my footstool" it follows that, if he is a man sitting in heaven, his shinbones have the length of the space between and earth.,' Bishop Diego replied.

The Cathars again affirmed that this was their interpretation and proceeded to argue their case from other texts, which Jordan does not record.

To modern ears all this seems very strange, but the two texts the Bishop used highlight the basic differences between Catholic and Cathar teachings.

As we have seen, the Cathars, in the Gnostic tradition, were unable to believe that a good God, who was a purely spiritual being, could create material things which were transient and perishable, and that, above all, he could create a world in which there was so much evil. Further, they saw all created, material things as evil, and so believed that there were two gods, the father in heaven, who is all good, and the god of this world, the creator, who had created the evil world. It is easy to see how attractive this belief would be to people who saw so much evil, sickness and suffering around them. It would not be easy to say that this world was created by a good God, in much the same way that many today, when faced with a natural catastrophe or terminal sickness, reject the idea of God.

Their belief was succinctly summed up by the Inquisitor Jacques Fournier, who in December 1334 became Pope Benedict X11. A learned theologian, as Inquisitor he had presided over the Inquisition at Pamiers and had gained an intimate knowledge, through his skilled questioning, of Cathar beliefs:

> There are two worlds, one visible, the other invisible. Each has its god. The invisible world has a good God, who saves souls. The other, the visible world, has an evil god who creates all visible and passing things . . . God created only spiritual beings, incorruptible and indestructible, for the works of God last for all

eternity; but all visible or sensible bodies, such as the sky, the earth and everything found upon it, with the sole exception of spirits, were made by the devil, the prince of the world; and because he made these things, they are all corruptible, for he can create nothing solid and lasting . . .

How can you say that God did not create my hands and my eyes? God has declared that nothing made by him can perish, for his Word, through whom he made all things, lives forever; and by this fact, nothing the Father has made can perish. And since everything in this visible world, the sky, the earth and all the creatures it contains, shall perish and be destroyed, it follows that he created none of them. It is the lord of this world who made them. God the Father, in fact, makes only what is good and speaks only what is good. Yet behold, there is much in this world that is evil, such as tempests, thunder and lightning. It is not God who made these, but his enemy, the prince of this world.[8]

Following on from this, the Cathars saw that the only way to attain true wisdom or 'gnosis' was to reject the material world in favour of a purely spiritual understanding of God. The Gospel of Saint John had a privileged place among them because they saw him as one of the 'enlightened' ones, which is strange, when Saint John

---

[8] Quoted in *Saint Dominic, The Grace of the Word*, Guy Bedouelle O.P. Ignatius Press 1987 P.173

specifically rejected their dualism and affirmed the reality of Jesus as Man, the Word made flesh.

Presumably their reply in the discussion was an acknowledgment that John was one who had attained true wisdom or 'gnosis'. Because the Gnostic tradition despised the body, the Cathar was probably referring to a spiritual body with his father in heaven, when acknowledging that his body stretched from heaven to earth rather the incongruous vision of 'a man sitting in heaven, his shinbones have the length of the space between heaven and earth.'

Catholic affirmation of the goodness of God's creation

Catholic teaching, on the contrary, affirms the goodness of creation. It affirms that Jesus Christ is the Son of Man—truly human—who has come down from heaven—truly divine. He was the Word made flesh. His Father is both the Creator God of the Old Testament and the Father supremely revealed in the New Testament. Gnostics and Cathars rejected the Old Testament as speaking of the evil creator god, and therefore would reject the story of creation, when God saw all that he had created and found it 'very good'. It is man's sin that brought evil into the world, and although this world is transient, as the Gnostics affirm, Catholics believe that nevertheless it has an eternal purpose because God has created it. Because the Second Person of the Blessed Trinity took flesh and became Man, then all of creation shares in the redemption he offers. It 'groans in travail in the meantime, awaiting the revealing of the sons of God' (cf Romans 8: 18-23), but it also shows forth the glory of God. We are encouraged to gaze in wonder at the beauty of the world and consider that if creation is so beautiful, then how much more wonderful is the God who made it. As Wisdom 13:3-5 says:

> If, charmed by such beauty, they took them for gods, let them know how far superior is their sovereign. And if they were impressed by their power and activity, let them understand from this how much mightier is he who formed them. For the grandeur and beauty of creatures leads us to ponder on their Author, greater and more magnificent.'

Debate at Servian

The first main town they reached was Servian, where they challenged the leading Albigensians, Baldwin and Thierry to a public debate, which lasted for eight days. They argued their cause to such effect that the townsfolk, listening to them, were won over completely and were reconciled to the Church. Unable to win the argument, Thierry, a nobleman from Northern France, remarked to the Bishop, 'I know of what spirit you are: you have come in the spirit of Elijah', to which the bishop replied that if he had come in the spirit of Elijah then Thierry had come in the spirit of the antichrist. Presumably, since the Cathars rejected the Old Testament, Thierry did not see Elijah in any positive light! The converted townsfolk, on the other hand, escorted them joyfully for more than a mile out of town when they left.

The preachers fanned out throughout the Langeudoc, although they did not always meet with such success.

Fanjeaux was a Cathar stronghold and was typical of a Cathar milieu. Meetings were held in the houses of members, not in churches; one of them at that time was a weaver's house kept by the *perfecti,* the Perfect, those who had received the *consolamentum,* or 'enlightenment', by the laying on of hands. They also owned a cobbler's shop and potteries.

Cathar Rituals and Hierarchy

Although Cathars rejected the Catholic system, and despite their rejection of the created world, they had a hierarchy and 'church' system of their own, and indeed called their sect a Church, the true, spiritual Church that proclaimed the true gospel and, in effect, set themselves up as a rival church. Cathar regions were divided into provinces, each with its own bishop with two assistants called—*filius maior* and *filius minor*—elder and younger son. When the bishop died the *filius maior* took his place. Each locality had its deacon. They had their own rituals and services. The *melioramentum* was a ritual veneration given by the ordinary Believers, the *credentes,* or the postulant seeking admission to the status of a *perfectus.* It consisted of three genuflections and a request for a blessing, 'Pray God to make a good Christian of me, and bring me to a good end.' The *Perfectus* would then bless him and say the prayer, 'May God make a good Christian of you and bring you to a good end.' There were elaborate rules for when to say the Lord's Prayer, a favourite with the Cathars, although lay Cathars were forbidden to say it, or to say the *double,* a prayer repeated twice. Their only obligation was to say the *melioramentum*

The men who had received the *consolamentum* became in effect the bishops. On receiving the *consolamentum* they put on a long black robe as a sign of their status and gave all their possessions to the church. They would then lead a wandering life of preaching, prayer and stringent fasting, and their emaciated faces and austerities earned them great respect from the Believers, or the ordinary Cathar faithful.

This peripatetic life was one factor of their success in gaining converts; they could travel long distances, preaching, establishing communities, which was in contrast with the existing Catholic religious who were mostly attached to their monasteries which were now far from where people were. If people wanted their spiritual guidance they had to go to them rather than the monks going to the people.

Trial by Fire

When Dominic and the Catholic party arrived in the town they agreed to a debate, even though the dispute was overseen by four judges who were all Cathars and therefore biased towards their opponents. They possibly came head to head with one of the most famous and respected Cathar preachers of the time, Guilhabert de Castres. Dominic spoke for the Catholic side but as the judges refused to concede that the Catholics were the clear winners they decided to put the result to the medieval 'trial by fire'. The book in which the texts Dominic had used were thrown into the fire three times and refused to burn, while that of the Cathars burnt up immediately.

A similar miracle was repeated at Montréal; Dominic had written on a sheet of paper quotations that he used in the disputation and gave it to one of the Cathars, asking him to read it and ponder on it. That evening, as the man sat by the fire with some friends they decided to put this paper to the 'trial by fire'. They thrust it into the fire three times, but each time the paper refused to burn. Even so, the Cathars were not won over either by Dominic's arguments or by this miracle and refused to be convinced and converted. Faith is a gift of God, and as Jesus Himself said, 'even if one were to rise from the dead they would not believe'.

Difficulty of Conversion

Even when the Cathars acknowledged that the Catholics had truth on their side they were not inclined to be reconciled to the Church. Bishop Foulques related that he had a discussion with a certain knight, Ponce Adhemar, who remarked that the Cathars did not realise that the Catholics had so many efficacious arguments against them, and acknowledged that they well knew that their own arguments were very weak.

'Then why do you not expel and banish them from your lands?' the bishop asked.

'We can't do that, since we were brought up among them,' Ponce Adhemar replied. 'We have relatives among them, and we see that they are living decently.'

The Cathar heresy was indeed deeply entrenched in the area and had been for perhaps a hundred years. In 1145 Saint Bernard himself had come to the region and reported with immense sorrow the state of the Church even in his time:

> The churches lack their congregations of
> the faithful; the faithful lack priests; and the
> priests lack all honour. All that remains are a
> few Christians without Christ. The sacraments
> are abused, and the Feasts of the Church are
> no longer celebrated. Men are dying with their
> sins still upon them. By refusing children the
> Grace of Baptism these people are depriving
> them of all life in Christ.

Saint Bernard preached his first sermon in the Cathedral
of Albi, in the heartland of Albigentianism, to a
congregation of only thirty people. Within two days the
Cathedral was too small to hold those who came to hear
him. Sadly, such fervour did not last, and in 1179 Pope
Alexander 111 launched a preaching crusade, which was
no more successful. Medieval Popes might popularly be
seen to be all-powerful potentates, but secular princes
could ignore them, promise their support then do
nothing; even bishops would ignore them unless they,
too, were as concerned as the pope about the state of their
dioceses.

Since Catharism was so entrenched, to convert could
split families apart, and many were not willing to take that
step. The Cathars were seen to live upright and decent
lives, they called themselves Christians, they called their
leaders 'Bons Hommes—good men—they quoted the
Gospels and prayed the Our Father; surely the beliefs on
which their goodness was based must be true, the ordinary
folk thought?

Since Cathar beliefs rejected the Church, the
sacraments, the priesthood, seeing all these as part of the
evil, material world, it therefore proved popular with

those who wanted to be free of the Church, especially the nobility. The Cathars had the support of the landed classes, who could exert their own power and influence in the region, free from ecclesiastical interference; the nobles had their own reasons for maintaining the Cathar status quo, which gave them far more freedom in their own domains, where the papal writ did not run. In addition, they gave protection to those who embraced the Cathar religion.

Another of the attractions of the Cathars was that women had a certain status in the sect, although they could not hold high office, and were often the ones who converted their menfolk. This was the age of the troubadour, a romantic movement that extolled women and which spread widely in the West, from Saint Francis of Assisi who sang in praise of his Lady Poverty, to Daffydd ap Gwilym, the renowned Welsh poet. The women of Languedoc had long been independently minded and found in the Cathar sect a religion that gave them more status than in the Catholic Church.

Gnosis

There was another, theological, reason for the Cathar success. Because the Cathars saw the Church and all its institutions and sacraments as part of the evil world, they also saw Catholics as inferior Christians who had to rely on these intermediaries between the soul and God. At the heart of the Gnostic tradition was the belief in the direct contact of the soul with God, a divine spark within, that had to be awaked by the *consolamentum*, the laying on of hands, which of itself conferred nothing since it was a physical gesture. Many who underwent this laying on of hands, though, testified that they experienced 'A transmission of immense vivifying energy'[9] passing into them, that assured them that they had attained enlightenment or 'gnosis'. It is an ironic paradox that the Cathars, who eschewed physical manifestations, should rely on this 'proof', whereas the Catholic Church, in evaluating a person's holiness, does not.

Catholic Response

Catholic theology does not deny that there is a 'divine spark', or rather, some presence of God within every human being and that God can act directly within a human soul, but this 'divine spark' is a pure gift of God who has made man in his own image and likeness, not something that he possesses in his own right, distinct from God. The Catholic Faith is incarnational; it is sacramental; that is, because the Word became flesh, the Church is now His body, his visible presence in the world. Because men and women are flesh and blood God uses the created world, water, bread, wine, oil, as vehicles of His grace, the invisible made visible, and men and women, who are pre-eminently the vehicles of His grace.

Throughout salvation history God has sent men and women to share in his work of redemption, to be 'ministers of the word'. Jesus Himself gave the commission to the disciples to go out into the whole world, baptising, teaching, with his own authority (cf. Matthew 28: 18-20)

---

[9]   Judith Mann quoted in *The Essence of the Gnostics*, Bernard Simon, Arcurus Press 2004 P.164

He sent out men and women to be his hands and feet and voice to others, and for men and women to be his presence in the world. For Dominic, this was his calling, to be a presence of God to the people, and to bring to them a true and deep understanding of their Catholic faith.

CHAPTER 3

PROUILLE

Besides the preaching missions, in the dilapidated little village of Prouille Bishop Diego set up another branch of activity that was no less important and would be even more far-reaching. The Cathars were so successful in gaining converts that in Prouille the Catholic presence had been reduced to poverty and despair. The Catholic nobility were forced to send their girls to Cathar convents for their education, with intense pressure to convert to that faith. The Cistercians had been successful in bringing back a few of them to the Faith, but there was nowhere for them to go to continue the life of dedication to God that had attracted them to Catharism in the first place. Then, nine young women came to the bishop and asked him to make provision for them to live a religious life. In 1206 Bishop Diego had a temporary house built for them and on the Feast of Saint Cecilia, 22 November 1206, the first nuns entered their convent and were clothed in the simple white tunic and black cloak that Dominic wore as an Augustinian. They would attend Mass at the nearby church of Our Lady of Prouille, which Bishop Foulques, the Cistercian Bishop of Toulouse, put at their disposal. Here, these young women could live their Catholic faith with at least as equal dedication as women *Perfectae* lived theirs. Don Diego put Guillemette of Fanjeaux, a Catholic noblewoman, in charge of the small community. Archbishop Berenger of Narbonne provided revenues for the young foundation, and Bishop Foulques gave it his whole-hearted support.

The Nuns of Prouille

Bishop Diego was now needed back in his own diocese, and so it fell to Dominic to be the father, the guide and the spiritual support for the young community. With Diego's admiration for the Cistercians it is likely that to begin with the nuns followed their rule of life. Theirs was a life of prayer, austerity and fervent intercession for the success of the missionaries, whom they supported with their contemplative prayer. It was inevitable, though, that they should be called on to instruct women in the Catholic faith, and to administer to the poor. They also helped support themselves with spinning the cloth for their own habits, and making altar cloths and vestments. In this they followed the example of the Cathar women who often used this industry to attract converts. As well, it was vital for them to provide an education for the Catholic young girls, because this was an aspect of Catharism that attracted women to them. If they could provide them with an education that until now was provided only by the Cathars, then the pressure to convert would be eased.

In a small and dilapidated house next to the monastery Dominic installed some priests who could act as the nuns' confessors and spiritual guides. It also provided a base for the priests as they fanned out systematically through the countryside, where they could return for rest, recuperation and brotherly support. However, this was not a religious community as such at this time. The priests were not bound to each other by any rule, only by a shared mission.

Sign from God

Dominic himself had received confirmation that all this was indeed blessed by God. One evening, he went up a steep hill between Prouille and Fanjeux, a larger town further up the hill from Prouille. Praying, he saw a ball of fire descending from heaven and circled several times over the town, settling for some time on the spire of the chapel of Notre Dame de Prouille. The same phenomenon recurred two following nights. The spot is now marked by a marble cross and is known by the name of Seignadou— sign of God.

The Rosary Tradition

This sign from the Mother of God marked the Order that Dominic founded with a special love for Mary; the nuns, as well, hold Prouille in special esteem as their spiritual home. Tradition has it that it was also at Prouille that Dominic gave his Order the Rosary as a special devotion, although the origins of the rosary stretch back much further than Dominic and its development had a long gestation. One legend states that Dominic was distressed that he was making so little progress with the Cathars and retired to a cave in woods near Toulouse, praying there for three days, when he received a vision of Our Lady. She appeared with three queens and fifty maidens, representing the rosary. She told him that for a gentle remedy for sickness, the rosary, not intellectual thundering against heresy, was required.

The legends linking Dominic with the rosary appear only 250 years after his death, and therefore scholars assume that there is no such link. However, the rosary was increasing in popularity during his time, though not in its present form. Beads had long been used to count the recitation of the *Ave Maria*. In Dominic's day this was made up only of what we know as the first half: 'Hail Mary, full of grace, the Lord is with you, blessed are you among women, and blessed is the fruit of your womb'. It was some two hundred years later that a Carthusian, Dominic of Prussia, attached meditations on the life of Christ to the recitation of the *Aves*.

Knowing of Dominic's deep love and devotion to the Mother of God it is surely perfectly reasonable to assume that Dominic would have used the devotion. At a deeper level, legends point to profound truths and this one is surely no exception. Dominic was totally devoted to Jesus, both God and Man, and saw how pernicious the Cathar belief was in denying that reality. In the rosary, the affirmation of the *Ave Maria,* 'blessed is the fruit of your womb', and the reality of the humanity of Jesus, born from the womb of Mary, threw down the gauntlet to the Cathars in their denial of the humanity of Jesus.

In contrast, Catholic belief affirms that in Jesus, God became man, the Word became flesh, and entered fully in all that makes us truly human. In prayer, we use our bodies in worship, and the beads of the rosary are a tangible aid to the bodily aspect of prayer; we use our voice when praying it with others; we engage our imagination in meditating on the various mysteries of Our Lord's life, and it can lead, as Saint Teresa of Avila said of the recitation of the Lord's Prayer, to the heights of contemplative prayer. In other words, the rosary engages the whole person in prayer. Even more, because the rosary draws us into the life of Jesus, from his Incarnation to his glorification in heaven and the glory of his Mother and all the saints, it anchors our prayer firmly into the life of the Incarnate Jesus, the Word made flesh, just as Dominic's whole spirituality was rooted in the humanity of Jesus.

In the words of Saint John of the Cross, 'If I have already told you all things in My Word, My Son, and if I have no other word, what answer or revelation can I now make that would surpass this? Fasten your eyes upon Him alone, because in Him I have spoken and revealed all, and in Him you shall discover even more than you ask for and desire'. (Ascent 11:22:5) Again, this was in contrast to the Cathars who saw nothing salvific in the earthly life of Jesus.

The rosary has always been specially connected with Our Lady, because she leads us into the presence of her Son, so it is no wonder that Dominic had a loving and tender relationship with her and would have revered this devotion. It is said that he began the custom of invoking the intercession of Our Lady by saying the prayer, '*Dignare me laudare te, Virgo sacrata*', allow me to praise you, holy Virgin'. What is evident is that the rosary fits perfectly into Dominican spirituality and was the best of spiritual weapons against Cathar heresy; it is deeply embedded within Dominican life. Four hundred years after Dominic's death they were successful in having the invocation 'Queen of the Most Holy Rosary' inserted into the Litany of Loreto.

Dominic's Way of Prayer

Just as the Rosary involves the whole person in prayer—words, often prayed aloud, the body, fingering the beads, the mind, praying the prayers and the soul united with God in meditation, in a similar way Dominic's prayer involved his whole being body and soul. He did not have the Cathar hatred of the body, who saw prayer as something purely 'spiritual' and rejected any outward aids to prayer, except for genuflections and prostrations. In the true tradition of Catholic spirituality Dominic used all the aids blessed by the Church, which recognises that we are human, given our bodies by God to be used in worship of him, even if, in moments of contemplative prayer we can pass beyond them.

As we have seen, Dominic loved to pray in church before the Blessed Sacrament. He would sometimes stand erect before the altar, his head bowed, wrapped in the mystery of Christ present before him or prostrate, outstretched on the ground. At other times he would remain kneeling before the altar, his gaze fixed on the crucifix, genuflecting frequently, sometimes praying out loud, or silently, his face often bathed in tears. At other times he would pray standing upright, his arms outstretched in the form of a cross; he would use this when interceding in prayer. He would pray with his arms raised to heaven as if drawing down the grace and blessings of heaven, or symbolic of his yearning for heaven. He knew the New Testament by heart, and would often be found meditating upon the Sacred Scriptures, with the book open on his lap. He prayed the Hours of the Office with the greatest devotion. On journeys he would often draw apart for prayer. Those who observed him could be in no doubt that his life was consumed by prayer.

Apostolic Labours

Bishop Diego returned to Osma in the Spring of 1207, leaving Dominic as priest in charge at Fanjeux and in charge of the preachers, while the Cistercian, William Claret, dealt with temporal matters. Sadly, Diego died suddenly in November of that year and Dominic lost a dear friend and guide. With the bishop's death most of the Cistercians also decided to return to their monasteries, because they had always felt that the active apostolate was not really compatible with their calling to the contemplative life. The Spanish priests whom Diego had left with Dominic also returned to their dioceses and for the next ten years Dominic was left to continue his apostolic activity almost alone, preaching throughout the region, with Prouille and Fanjeux as his base. It was not an easy time for him, because he faced the anger, mockery and often physical attacks on his life from the Cathars, even though they did not believe in waging war or in violence. When they threatened to kill him he replied calmly that he was not worthy of the martyr's glory, 'as yet I have not merited such a death.' When he was asked why he remained in the Carcassonne diocese, where he was treated so badly, rather than in the Toulouse diocese, 'Because in the Toulouse diocese I find many persons who pay me honour,' he replied, 'but in Carcassonne everyone attacks me.'

The Cathars treated him as a fool. They spat on him, threw mud and stones at him, they tried everything they could think of to humiliate him, but he responded to their attacks with humility. Even when he knew he might be walking into an ambush where his life would be at stake, he showed no fear. He simply walked on boldly, singing psalms and hymns at the top of his voice. This so disconcerted them that they eventually asked him what he would do if he were ambushed. 'I would not want you to kill me quickly or easily,' he replied. He longed to die the most horrible death they could conceive, for love of God. He was left alone after that.

Giving an Example of Humility

At one time a big conference was held in the district and a bishop from a neighbouring diocese arrived with a sumptuous retinue, which horrified Dominic. He explained that such a display of secular pomp would earn the derision of the Cathars. 'My father,' he said, 'this isn't the way we have to behave with this proud generation. We have to convince these enemies to the truth by the example of humility and patience rather than by the pomp and grandeur of worldly show. Let us arm ourselves with prayer and humility and go barefoot against these Goliaths.' The bishop and his retinue humbly took off their shoes and walked with Dominic to the conference in their bare feet. At one point they lost their way and asked directions from a passerby. The man turned out to be a Cathar, and he led the party through ground covered with stones and briars so that their feet were cut and lacerated, their legs running with blood. This was of little moment to one like Dominic who longed to be a martyr for Christ's sake, and who for long had voluntarily mortified himself so as to resemble his suffering Lord. He cheerfully encouraged his more timid companions and so impressed the Cathar with his patience and example that he was converted.

Dominic did not parade his austerity, but recognised that when austerity was so prized by the Cathars he could perhaps win them over by example. One Lent he and a few of his companions received hospitality from a noble family in Toulouse that had embraced the Cathar cause, and began to win them over by more austerity than their Cathar hosts could manage. They lived only on bread and water throughout Lent and slept on table tops, rising early to keep vigil in prayer. They asked their host for clothing and when he asked them what they needed, replied, hair shirts, adding, 'But keep it a secret and don't let anyone know.' They won the admiration of their hosts for their eminent holiness, and they gradually began to be drawn back toward the Catholic faith.

Dominic always fasted on bread and water during Lent, and it was observed that he ended in better health than at the beginning.

Body and Spirit

The Cathars were no strangers to mortification and austerity, but for far different reasons than Dominic's. The rejection of the world by the Cathars arose from their contempt for the world God had made, whereas Dominic embraced the cross in whichever form it came for love of Christ. Although he did not have the great love for nature that Francis of Assisi had, he never rejected anything that the good God whom he adored and worshipped had made.

Rejection of Marriage

Seeing all material things as evil, Cathars rejected marriage, preferring co-habitation. While marriage was tolerated among ordinary believers, they taught that no married couples would be saved after death; once they were inducted into the ranks of the Perfect they would have to renounce their marriage. Childbearing and sexual intercourse was considered sinful, so the logical and deadly consequence of this, if the Cathar sect was ever to infiltrate society totally, and all became Perfects, would be the destruction of the human race. However, while their followers remained among the ordinary believers they could bear children.

This had an added advantage for the women. They could live the life of the ordinary Believer while they were of child-bearing age, bear children to be brought up in the Cathar faith, and then, once they hade fulfilled that duty they could then renounce their marriage, be enrolled in the ranks of the Perfect and enjoy the prestige, the freedom and the status this brought with it.

The Cathars rejected marriage because, according to their beliefs, the flesh imprisoned the 'divine spark' that originated in heaven, either as a fallen angelic being or as a reincarnated soul, in a yet even more degraded existence. The divine spark could only be released to its former beatitude through the coming of Jesus, not truly as man but as an angelic being, a phantom, in the semblance of man. He did not truly die on the cross, only showed the way back to heaven by means of the *consolamentum*. It followed, then, that those who gave birth to a child were co-operating in imprisoning a soul; on the other hand, any form of sexual practice, apart from marriage, was legitimate and preferable.

Because they abhorred the sexual act, even in animals, they were vegetarian, abstaining from meat, eggs and dairy products, because animals were the products of sexual reproduction. However, they ate fish because it was believed that fish were not the product of sexual reproduction. Because of the severity of their rejection of all that made human living tolerable, the Perfect would often undergo the *endura,* or suicide by starvation or the administration of poison at the end of their lives, in order to enter the afterlife untainted by anything pertaining to the world.

Athlete of Christ

Dominic's austerity differed from that of the Cathars by the intent behind it. Dominic was dubbed 'the athlete of Christ' for his indefatigable missionary journeys, but also because he shared Saint Paul's vision of 'fighting the good fight and winning the race'. Just as an earthly athlete subjected himself to a rigorous routine and disciplined his body in order to win an earthly prize, so, Paul said, he 'buffeted his body to bring it under submission. This is what Dominic did in his turn, bringing his body under control so that he was stripped and ready, as it were, for anything the Lord wanted him to do. At a deeper level, he would echo the words of Saint Paul that he was making up, in his own body, the sufferings that were lacking in the sufferings of Christ, longing to unite himself totally with the cross of Christ.

The Resurrection

Another source of great concern to Dominic in his disputes with the Cathars was that they did not believe in the death and resurrection of Christ. Because the belief that Jesus, the Son of the good God, had taken flesh in the womb of the Virgin Mary was totally abhorrent to them, they believed that Jesus was an angel sent from the Father, that he took on only the appearance of a man, and that he only appeared to die. This is logical to their thinking, since they saw all material things as evil, and of course Jesus did not belong to the evil world. It meant, therefore, that they put the Cross of Christ to nought and saw salvation as something attained by 'gnosis', wisdom, not something won for us by the cross and resurrection of Jesus.

Although they did not believe in the resurrection they did believe in reincarnation, so that those who had not achieved the perfection of 'knowledge' in their lifetime would return to another try, as it were. However, there was a downside. One who had led a just life would be reincarnated into a better body, but one who had led a sinful life would be reincarnated into a worse one, or even into that of an animal, in a downward spiral that could not be halted unless a messenger came down from the good god on their behalf.

Dominic had such a profound understanding and transforming experience of the saving grace of Jesus in his own life, such a deep love for his beloved Lord, that it wounded him deeply that the Cathars could so easily set aside what Jesus had done for them at such great cost. He would often urge his brothers to 'think about our Saviour'. Not simply think about Jesus, but think about him in his work of salvation and what he had brought to them in his saving work and renewal, in the transformation of lives, in heaven already begun and ever in progress.

Miracles

However bereft of human support Dominic had during this period in Fanjeux, there are many stories of divine aid that he had. In 1211, he came across a band of forty English pilgrims by the bank of the Garonne, bound for Compostella. Since at that time the nearby city of Toulouse was under interdict, and therefore they would not be able to participate in the Mass there, they hired a boat to take them across the river. The boat, small and overloaded, capsized in the middle of the river and the terrified pilgrims were in danger of drowning. Dominic was praying in a small church nearby but was alerted by the cries of those who had witnessed the accident. By that time most of the pilgrims had disappeared from sight, feared already drowned. Dominic prostrated himself in prayer, then stood up and called out loudly, 'I command you in the name of the Lord Jesus Christ to come to the shore alive and unhurt!' Immediately the drowning pilgrims came to the surface and all made their way safely to the shore.

Another time Dominic accidentally dropped his precious books in a river as he was crossing it on foot. Three days later a fisherman drew them out of the water completely undamaged. Another time, Dominic had no money to pay for his fare when a boatman had taken him across a river. The man threatened to take his cloak as payment, so Dominic laid the cloak on the ground, prayed, and then pointed silently to a silver piece lying on it. 'My brother,' he said, 'there is what you ask. Take it, and let me go on my way.'

CHAPTER 4

WAR, INQUISITION, CRUSADE

The following year things took a more ominous turn in the region. On 14 January 1208, one of the legates, Peter of Castelnau, was assassinated on the banks of the Rhone, with the tacit approval of the lord of the region, Count Raymond of Toulouse. The Count was a colourful and contradictory character; he had been married five times, with two divorced wives still living. He systematically persecuted the churches and monasteries in his domain, and when he attended Mass did so only to parody the gestures of the priest and mock the sacred liturgy. On the other hand, he showed utmost reverence to the Cathar bishops and dignitaries. His contemporaries described him as 'a limb of Satan, a child of perdition, a hardened criminal, a parcel of sinfulness', and Pope Innocent was no less complimentary, calling him 'an impious, cruel tyrant, creature both pestilent and insane.' However, on the death of Peter he was treated as a hero.

Peter of Castelnau, a Cistercian monk of the Abbey of Fontfroide who had been Archdeacon of Maguelonne, had earned the hatred of the Cathars by his harshness and severity, asserting that religion would never raise its head in Languedoc until it was watered by the blood of a martyr—although his prayer was that it would be his. His prayer was answered after he had excommunicated Count Raymond of Toulouse. Members of the Count's household ambushed and killed him in the early hours of 15 January 1208. Until then, Pope Innocent 111 had tried all peaceful means of trying to persuade the Count to restore order to his territories, and to restore orthodox Christianity, but this atrocity changed everything. Four years earlier, the Pope had reluctantly come to the conclusion that sterner measures were needed, a Crusade against the heretics. On 10 March 1204 he wrote to the King of France: 'It is your responsibility to harry the Count of Toulouse out of those lands which at present he occupies; to remove this territory from the control of sectarian heretics; and to place it in the hands of true Catholics who will be enabled, under your beneficent rule, to serve our Lord in all faithfulness.' However, the secular powers were in no hurry to support the Pope, and the persecution of Catholics and the despoliation of their property continued. One man defiled a church altar, others desecrated Communion chalices and crucifixes. The Count of Foix seized a priest and hacked him to pieces. Such attacks on the clergy were by no means rare, whipped up by the anti-clerical bias of the Cathars' preaching. In the face of such atrocities the Pope felt he had to take sterner measures.

Inquisition?

Dominic's reputation has been linked with two ways by which the Church combated heresy, the Inquisition and the Albigensian Crusades. What is the truth behind the often harsh criticisms levelled at him, and subsequently at the Dominican Order?

Was Dominic the founder of the Inquisition, as is often alleged? What was the position of the Church when Dealing with Heresy? Because the excesses of the Spanish Inquisition have left such a dark stain in the folk memory of the West, it is necessary to suggest a more balanced approach. Indeed, documents from that period that are now being studied are leading to a better understanding of the workings of the Inquisition, even though its cruelty under such figures as Torquemada cannot be denied.

Dealing with heresy

From the very beginning the Church has had to deal with heresy, as even the New Testament writings attest. Jesus Christ Himself gave his authority to the Church to preach the Gospel in His name—'All authority in heaven and earth has been given to me. Go, therefore, and teach all nations.' (Matthew 28). The Acts of the Apostles and the letters of Paul, John and James witness to how boldly this commission was carried out, and at the same time how careful they were to preach only what Christ had commanded them. If members of the Church dissented from the teaching of the apostles, then they were excluded from Church fellowship. The early Church Fathers upheld freedom of conscience, and therefore that religious belief could not be imposed by force or dissent punished by torture or death. After Constantine, it was the secular authorities who began to impose penalties and even death, much against the wishes of the bishops and teachers of the Church, such as Augustine. Sometimes, as in Liège in 1144, it was the mob that took matters into their own hands and the Cathars were saved only by the intervention of the bishop and priests, or when the clergy were unable to save them as in the case of the Cathars of Cologne.

As we have already seen, the Pope wanted to persuade rather than punish. At the 4th Lateran Council in 1215 Pope Gregory, in his anti-heresy decrees, adhered to the principle of *ecclesia abhorret a sanguine*—the Church abhors the shedding of blood—even though in the decree he equated heresy with treason against the state, which did carry the death sentence. In that era there was no separation of Church and State; society was a Christian society in which Christian values worked in conjunction with the secular authorities. However, when the Emperor Frederick 11 began hounding heretics on his own behalf and in 1224 made heresy punishable by death, the Pope had to respond by appointing a special commission to ensure that such matters should remain under the authority of the Church, and to ensure that those accused had the charges against them properly investigated and not subjected to the often arbitrary, secular, justice of the time.

The Inquisition

No, Dominic was not involved in the Inquisition. The tribunal, or inquisition, was set up in 1231, after his death, and it was mostly the Franciscans, as well as the Dominicans, who were given the authority to examine suspected heretics as to their doctrinal beliefs. The Church never had the authority to execute a death sentence, although it did hand over to the secular powers those convicted of heresy, and could therefore be seen as complicit in the death sentence.

Qualities of an Inquisitor

The charge given to the religious orders in this role was daunting. Two inquisitors, Bernard Gui and Eymeric, laid out the qualities that the inquisitor should possess: he should, in a pre-eminent degree, possess the qualities of a good judge; he should be animated with a glowing zeal for the Faith, the salvation of souls and the extirpation of heresy; amid all the difficulties and dangers he should never yield to anger or passion; he should meet hostility fearlessly, but should not court it; he should yield to no inducement or threat, and yet not be heartless. When circumstances permitted, he should observe mercy in allotting penalties; he should listen to the counsel of others, and not trust too much to his own opinion or to appearances, since often the probable is untrue and the truth improbable. Gregory 1X himself stated that 'they should not so punish the wicked as to harm the innocent.' A high standard indeed, and so it is no wonder, as recent research has shown, that accused persons often preferred to be tried by an ecclesiastical court rather than the much harsher and more arbitrary secular courts.

Inevitably, human nature being what it is, some inquisitors and some Cathars alike overstepped the mark. The violence was not always on the Catholic side, as has often been portrayed. The friars were beaten up and driven from Toulouse at one point; some were murdered, their convents sacked and destroyed. Cathars eschewed violence and war, but usually employed others to persecute the Catholics on their behalf. Their leaders also came up with another justification for killing Catholics: since it was legitimate to kill those given over to the devil, and since Catholics were obviously on the side of the devil, then they could legitimately be killed.

On the Catholic side some inquisitors did overstep the mark. Often, the worst perpetrators were those who had converted from Catharism themselves, such as Robert le Bougre, who had nearly two hundred heretics burnt at the stake in 1239. However, when Pope Gregory heard of le Bougres' activities he immediately removed him from office and imprisoned him for life.

A bizarre and disturbing incident occurred 4 August 1225, which was very far from Dominic's spirit. It was a few months after Dominic had been canonised and the Dominicans in Toulouse were celebrating his first feastday. The Bishop, Raymond du Fauga, finished celebrating Mass and was due to join them for a meal when he received the news that the mother-in-law of Peytavi Borsier, a well-known Believer living nearby, had been given the *consolamentum*. The bishop, with several of the friars hurried to the house and the old lady, who was dying, received him happily, believing that he was the Cathar bishop. Raymond du Fauga did not disillusion her, but encouraged her to affirm her commitment to Catharism, then, revealing his identity, urged her to abjure her beliefs. This she firmly refused to do, and the local magistrate who judged her to be a heretic, ordered her to be carried out on her bed and burned. The friars and bishop then returned cheerfully to their convent for the feast.

That the friars rejoiced at this turn of events is disturbing. It must be noted, though, that they were not directly involved in the incident. It was the bishop who interrogated the woman, and the magistrate who ordered her execution. There is one possibility to be considered. Believers often delayed receiving the *consolamentum* until they were near death, as this lady was, and then undergo the *endura*, that is, end their life so that they would enter the afterlife without sin. Was this the reason why the magistrate ordered her execution, so that she would not be encouraged to commit suicide?

Peter of Verona

Dominicans later became the most notable of the inquisitors, and one of the most famous was Peter of Verona. Born in 1206 of a Cathar family of Verona, he was sent first to a Catholic school and then to the University of Bologna, when at the age of fifteen he met Saint Dominic. He was sent to preach throughout Italy and won many converts from Catharism, but he was also stern against those Catholics who professed the faith but whose deeds and way of life did not match their words. He was 46 years of age when he was appointed Inquisitor in Lombardy, where his only recorded act was a declaration of clemency for those who confessed or were sympathetic to heresy. He filled this role for only six months when he was murdered by Carino of Balsamo and Manfredo Clitoro of Guissino, who had been hired by some Milanese Cathars. They chopped the top of his head off with an axe, and his last words were to begin to recite the Apostles Creed, and becoming the Order's first martyr. He was canonised the following year, and his assassin Carino later confessed to the crime, was converted, and ended his days as a Dominican lay brother, being venerated locally as Blessed Carino of Balsamo.

Crusade

What of Dominic's involvement in the Crusade when the Pope decided to send an army into the Languedoc to restore order? Count Raymond, sensing that things would be coming to a head very soon, had been quietly massing troops and fortifying his strongholds for a coming conflict, but conveniently switched sides and supported the Pope's forces for the time being. It is easy to see the Albigensian Crusade as the Church's brutal suppression of heresy, but the Pope's concerns were to a great extent well founded. Territories held by the Cathars and Albigensians were descending into anarchy. The Pope had long been concerned, not only with the ravages of the heresy but also with the increasing lawlessness that the Count seemed unwilling to confront in his territory. In reality, the two problems were linked, one factor being that the Cathars rejected the taking of oaths. In the medieval period oaths were of paramount importance in guaranteeing the stability of the state and of daily life; so to repudiate the taking of oaths was yet another threat, in addition to other areas of Cathar belief, which threatened the stability of the state.

Sieges of Beziers and Carcassone

Having decided on a crusade, the Pope asked the French king, Philip Augustus, to organise it. With the king engaged in a war with the English at the time, it took him nearly a year to organise an army, and the first siege, that of Beziers, which lasted for only an hour, was disastrous for the reputation of the Catholic army. Poorly led, and with a ragtag of soldiers and mercenaries, when the town fell the soldiers ran riot, raping, looting and murdering all they laid hands on. It was said that when Simon de Montfort—other sources say the Papal Legate—was asked how they could distinguish between Catholic and Cathar, he was alleged to have replied 'Kill them all; God will know his own'. This myth has been traced to a German monk of very doubtful credentials and a bright imagination, one Caesarius of Heisterbach, writing some sixty years after the event.[10]

Soon after, Carcassone, also fell to the crusaders. Horrified by the way in which victory had been won, the leaders then held a council to decide who should remain in charge of the captured territory. It was a delicate undertaking, because it involved taking over feudal lands owned by the Count of Toulouse, and therefore considered by some to be illegal. Nevertheless, Simon de Montfort, Earl of Leicester, was offered the position and was pressed to accept it. With the tendency of the nobility to switch sides or renege on their promises, Simon accepted only on the condition that the leaders of the Crusade should swear to support him if he needed them.

---

[10] Vid. Régine Pernould, *Those Terrible Middle Ages,* Ignatius Press, 2000, P.18

Simon de Montfort

At the time it was a wise choice. The second son of Simon and Amicia of Leicester, Simon de Montfort had succeeded to the earldom in 1181 on the death of his father and elder brother, although King John seized his lands in England and refused to acknowledge his right to the earldom. However, Simon owned extensive lands in Normandy, having descended from the lords of Montfort l'Amaury. He was an astute and capable strategist, always leading from the front, and with a charismatic flair for leadership. More importantly, he had a deep faith. He had learnt his skills of war in the Fourth Crusade, but he had refused to take part in attacking his fellow Christians in Byzantium. Given the debacle of Beziers, he could perhaps win the hearts and minds of the people, while at the same time capturing other towns and cities in the region—Limoux and Albi (the heartland of the Albigensians), and seizing the fortress towns of Minerve, Termes and Cabaret.

In 1209 Simon made his headquarters in Fanjeux, moving there with his family. They soon became close friends with Dominic, who baptised Simon's daughter Petronella, and performed the marriage ceremony of Simon's son Amaury. Another of his daughters, Amicia, would in time found the Dominican monastery of Montargis, and became its Prioress.

Simon contributed generously to the financial upkeep of Dominic's preaching mission, and also helped fund the monastery at Prouille. Dominic found in Simon a man after his own heart—deeply Catholic, courageous, with a strong personality. A contemporary chronicler, William of Tudela, described him as 'this wealthy, doughty and valiant lord, this hardy warrior, full of wisdom and experience, a great and gentle knight, gallant, comely, frank yet gently spoken.'

Dominic's Role as Comforter

Dominic accompanied Simon at the siege of Lavour and at the capture of La Penne d'Ajen, at Pamiers and Muret, at Simon's request; the only recollection people had of Dominic was his untiring efforts to bring help and succour to the women and children, the aged and the infirm, saving as many of them as he could. Dominic's vocation was to preach and teach the Faith, not to take up arms for it. A painting in the monastery of St Sixtus, the Order's house in Rome, attests to this. It shows Dominic studying, with a dog at his feet holding a candle, and another friar chasing a dog with a stick. The inscription explains that Dominic opposed the devil not with violence but with study, and it could equally be said that he confronted heresy not with the sword but with prayer.

Battle of Muret

This was brought out strongly in the battle of Muret. The Albigensian army had been greatly strengthened by the arrival of Peter, King of Aragon, with a large army at his back. The Albigensians now vastly outnumbered the Catholic forces, and the Catholics decided to hold a Council of war at Muret. Dominic made his way there, but on September 10 the King of Aragon suddenly arrived at the gates of the town, taking Simon de Montfort by surprise. The King refused to negotiate a truce, and battle was inevitable. The Albigensian army now numbered forty thousand, the Catholic defenders a mere eight hundred. Simon knew there was no hope for the Catholic army and prepared to sell his life dearly. Just before the battle he knelt before the Bishop of Toulouse and vowed, 'I consecrate my blood and life for God and His faith.'

They rode out to battle, and the Bishop with his priests and the women went into the church to pray. Dominic urged them to pray the rosary. Fortified by the prayers Simon proved himself a resourceful and inspired tactician. Riding out through the open gates of the town, Simon and his troops pretended to retreat, then reversed suddenly, driving through the massed ranks of the Albigensians to where Peter of Aragon was, surrounded by his nobles, and killed him. Demoralised, his army fled, leaving the field to the victorious Catholics. Truly a miraculous victory.

Rebellion

Having conquered the territory from Raymond of Toulouse, who in the meantime had switched sides, Simon was appointed Count of Toulouse and Duke of Narbonne at the Council of Montpellier, which had been convened in January 1207, to decide on measures that would bring some stability to the region. To begin with, Simon was popular, and town after town opened up to him, but ambition, and the precarious support of the nobles who gradually melted away, left him vulnerable. This gradually perverted his judgment and he became more and more cruel and intransigent in his governance of the lands under his control, earning the undying hatred of the French.

When rebellion broke out in Provence Simon marched to Toulouse, which had been occupied by Raymond of Toulouse's son, to besiege it. He seemed to have had some premonition that he would die during the assault, for he attended Mass, and when messengers came to him urgently to engage the assault he responded, 'Allow me to partake of the Divine Mysteries first, and look upon the Holy Sacrament, the pledge of our salvation.' With the battle becoming fiercer another messenger arrived, saying that the men would not be able to sustain the brunt of it much longer without him. Simon again responded, 'I shall not come forth until I have looked upon my Redeemer.' At the elevation of the Chalice he raised his arms, recited the *Nunc* Dimittis, and then rose, saying 'Come then, and if we must; let us die for Him who deigned to die for us.'

The city was defended mostly by women and children, and he died when a stone launched from a mangonel, a stone-throwing siege engine operated by some women, smashed into his skull. He died 24 June 1218, a sad end for someone who had shown such promise, and the degradation of a once noble character, who yet still retained his faith to the end.

If, in French eyes, Simon de Montfort's reputation was destroyed, in contrast Dominic so endeared himself to the people during this dangerous time, and assured as they were of his holiness, he was variously asked to be bishop of Beziers, of Comminges and of Navarre, but he steadfastly refused. He said that he would rather take flight in the night, with only his staff, than accept a bishopric.

Conversion of Pons Roger

It was about this time, 1208, that Dominic won a notable convert, Pons Roger of Tréville, in the Lauraguais district. He was a noted Albigensian 'Perfect', and in one of the only three extant letters written by Dominic to the Cistercian Legate, he sets out the conditions of life he had to follow. On three Sundays or on major feasts, he was to be marched to the church while a priest flogged him. He was to fast rigorously, except on Easter Sunday, Pentecost and Christmas, wear religious clothes, embrace chastity, attend Mass daily and say the Divine Office and a set number of the 'Our Father' daily. This might seem harsh, but as a commentator has pointed out,[11] such an austere life was but a reflection of the austerity of life he would have lived as a 'Perfect'. To live a less austere life as a Catholic would have implied that he had to live a less ascetical life in the true Church. But as a Catholic, he could live a no less fervent life, but one inspired now by the love of God. By forbidding him to fast on the great Feasts of the Church, Dominic was affirming that his fasting was not to be done as an expression of contempt for the body and the physical world, but as a loving sacrifice to the good God who gave his life for us, and in union with that sacrifice.

Dominic at Toulouse

Such conversions were few and far between, though, and during these years a far different future was forming in

---

[11]   *Saint Dominic, Biographical Documents*, note 12 p. 255

Dominic's mind, which was soon to take shape. In 1210 he went to Toulouse on a preaching mission at the request of his old friend Bishop Foulques. In 1213 Bishop Guy of Carcassone, who had been be absent from his diocese for a while, appointed him as Vicar General of Carcassone and he preached the Lenten services that year. On Bishop Guy's return, Bishop Foulques appointed Dominic parish priest of Fanjeaux, which had in any case been his base for several years. In 1211 Toulouse had been placed under interdict and excommunication because of a rebellion by the Count of Toulouse in favour of the Albigensians, and all the clergy and religious had to leave the city until the bans were lifted in 1214. The Council of Montpellier, recognising the quality of the two men, requested both Bishop Foulques and Dominic to come to Toulouse to evangelise the diocese.

Dominic returned to the city in April 1215 with some brothers who had, over the years, joined him in his preaching mission. They were to be the nucleus of a new and revolutionary Order, the fulfilment of Dominic's prayers and dreams. Jesus spent thirty years of 'hidden life' before he began his short public ministry. Dominic was now forty six years of age, and in a similar way his 'hidden years', those long years of silent preparation, were coming to fruition, and his God-given and enduring work was about to begin

CHAPTER 5

THE FRIARS PREACHERS

On his arrival in Toulouse Dominic and his six companions were met by two wealthy citizens of the city, Peter Seila and a man called Thomas, who placed themselves and their wealth at his disposal. Peter Seila offered them three of his own houses by the Narbonne Gate, and Dominic accepted the largest of them. It was there, in the first convent of the Order of Preachers, that Dominic clothed the first friars in the habit he himself already wore—a white woollen tunic, a surplice of linen and a hooded mantle of black. He introduced his companions to the religious life of prayer and poverty, and also of study. Dominic intended his Order to be devoted to preaching the Word of God, for they could not give to others what they did not possess themselves.

His great friend Bishop Diego had died, but in the Bishop of Toulouse, Bishop Foulques, he found another great friend and one who supported him totally in his work for souls. Foulques had succeeded to the diocese in 1206 when his predecessor, Raymond de Rabastens, had been deposed for simony. As an example of the equivocal stance of the clergy, Raymond came from a strongly Cathar family, and Foulques found the episcopal coffers empty because Raymond had spent all the money on fighting his vassals. He was even hounded by Raymond's creditors for overdue debts. Coming from a family of businessmen the Bishop wasted no time in setting his ruined diocese in order.

Bishop Foulques

The Bishop was himself an interesting character. He was born about 1150, and came from a Genoese merchant family from Marseilles. Married with two sons, he was wealthy in his own right; a contemporary described him as renowned for his spouse, his progeny and his home. He was also a renowned troubadour, celebrated by Dante. However, in 1195 he gave all that up when he entered the Catholic Church. He placed his wife and sons in monastic institutions before himself entering the Cistercian Order and became Abbot of Thoronet. As abbot he helped found a sister house at Gémémos, where his wife entered. His sons, Ildephonsus and Petrus, entered the Cistercian abbey of Grandselves where both became abbots. The fact that he was known as 'the Devil's Bishop' by his enemies testifies to his success in restoring a Catholic heart to his diocese, and found in Dominic a man after his own heart. The only difference of opinion they had was that Bishop Foulques supported an armed crusade, whereas Dominic favoured conversion by prayerful persuasion through debate and informed preaching.

Foulques was therefore delighted with the brothers, and put aside one-sixth of the tithes of his diocese to support them. He also signed a charter approving their congregation, and made all of the brothers official preachers in his diocese. The bishop's enthusiastic approval, the gift of a house, were signs to Dominic that he was following God's will, and now he received another. Alexander Stavensby, a renowned doctor of theology at the University, fell asleep over his books early one morning, and dreamt that he saw seven stars that grew ever brighter. The following morning Dominic and his six companions arrived at his lecture dressed in their black and white habits. They said that they were poor brothers who wanted to preach the Gospel to all the inhabitants of Toulouse, Catholic and Cathar alike, but wanted to learn from him first. Alexander recognised the prophetic nature of his dream and later was proud to have been the first Master of the Friars Preachers.

The 4th Lateran Council

In the autumn of that year Bishop Foulques took Dominic with him to Rome to attend the opening of the Fourth Lateran Council, 11 November 1215, called by Innocent 111. Innocent, a charming, wise and witty ruler, perhaps embodied the apex of both the secular and spiritual power in the history of the Church. In his Office of Pope, he considered that the secular realm was subordinate to the spiritual realm, and used his authority to curb the ambitions of princes, including England's King John, and authorised the Crusade in the Holy Land. On the other hand, his primary concern was for the pastoral care of his flock, and even though the Lateran Council met for only three weeks it instigated widespread reforms—obliging the faithful to go to confession and communion at least once a year, reforming the marriage laws and the monasteries, and laws to regulate the discharge of episcopal duties, for example. Above all, he wanted the preaching of the Gospel to be done with sound teaching, and in the language of the people.

Apart from the importance of this Council for the life of the Church, for Dominic it was an opportunity for advancing the fortunes of his Order. Bishop Foulques had the authority to approve the Order as a diocesan establishment, but by obtaining Papal approval Dominic was already looking ahead to something far more widespread and influential. He knew that the Pope had already shown his deep concern over the advance of heresy and civil disorder, especially in France and Spain. Despite the success of the Albigensian campaign in restoring some semblance of order, the Pope was under no illusion that force alone could counter heresy. It needed persuasion, intelligent discussion, above all the action of the Holy Spirit, to change hearts and minds. When, therefore, Dominic came to him with his plans to found an Order devoted to preaching the Gospel of Christ he met with a sympathetic ear but initially with some reservations, because this was indeed a novel proposal. Nevertheless, the Pope had the breadth of vision to see the value of Dominic's new Order. Besides Dominic, he had also already seen, beneath Francis of Assisi's ragged and uncouth appearance, another gift from God for the reform of the Church. In these two men he had the example of the high holiness he needed. To both of them he became a supportive friend and a true father in God.

Proclamation of the Gospel

The reason why Dominic's vision was so revolutionary was that since apostolic times the public proclamation of the Gospel was the responsibility of bishops, who had the authority to licence and delegate the ministry to the priests, secular and religious, under his pastoral care. In the religious ferment of the times there were many enthusiasts, wandering preachers and reformers without authorisation, who also went round preaching an often dubious form of the Christian message, and were, almost to a man, anti-clerical. Ordained priests were too often lazy, ill-educated and too ill-informed to provide the sound teaching for which their people yearned and that they desperately needed. Innocent 111 saw in Dominic and his companions, in their bare feet and patched habits, an answer to his prayers.

At first, the Pope was disconcerted by Dominic's proposal for an order of preachers that did not look to a bishop for authorisation, but soon approved and placed the convent of Prouille under his own protection. One of the reasons was that many of the bishops were not capable of preaching themselves, and the Pope felt that they would be greatly helped to have qualified men to take over the role.

Dominic and Francis Meet

The Fourth Lateran Council was also the occasion of the meeting between Saint Francis and Saint Dominic, two kindred souls who loved and served God with all their hearts. Tradition has it that the two saints exchanged the girdles around their waists; Dominic gave Francis the leather girdle of the preacher, and Francis gave Dominic the knotted rope that denoted the poverty of his Order. It is also said that Dominic attended the Chapter of Mats, a meeting of the brethren of the Franciscan Order, with so many attending that many of the friars had to sleep outdoors on roughly woven mats. It is also said that Dominic was horrified when, after an inspiring address by Francis, he realised that Francis had made no provision for feeding so many men. Then, in the distance, he saw townsfolk approaching the site of the chapter laden with provisions for the brethren. Although Dominic loved and embraced poverty for himself, he was also a wise and competent organiser, but recognised a lesson in abandonment to the providence of God, not only for himself, but also for his own followers.

Deciding the Dominican Rule

Dominic returned home in January the following year with the papal approval, but with one proviso, that he should discuss with his brothers which Rule they wished to adopt, and then return to obtain the papal approbation. There were so many new religious movements springing up that the Pope had stipulated that no new Rules could be drawn up. Any new Orders had to adopt one of the existing Rules.

They returned to Toulouse and Dominic found that their numbers had grown to sixteen. There was Thomas and Peter, who had put their wealth and themselves at Dominic's disposal. Matthew of Paris was the eldest among this group of young men, and whose wisdom Dominic cherished. The band already reflected the international nature of the Order, and gave an insight in the way Dominic drew men to himself. Bertrand of Garrigua, Brother Noel of Prouille, Brother Dominic the Second and Brother John of Navarre had been his constant companions during his preaching tours. William

Claret of Panders was a Cistercian who perhaps stayed with Dominic when the other Cistercians returned to their monasteries. He made his profession with Dominic, but returned to the Cistercians in 1224. Michael of Fabra and Michael of Uzero had been with Bishop of Diego. Suiero Gomez, a nobly born Portugese had been in Simon de Montfort's army and had witnessed the miraculous rescue of the English pilgrims, and Lawrence the Englishman had been one of those rescued. Like Bertrand, Stephen of Metz, a Belgian, shared Dominic's love of austerity and zeal for souls. There was Oderic of Normandy, a laybrother, and Dominic's own brother, Mannes.

Dominic called a meeting at Prouille, where they discussed which Rule they wished to adopt. It was agreed unanimously to adopt the Rule of Saint Augustine, which Dominic had already been following for many years. It was perhaps the shortest of all the Rules at that time, and was more a treatise of exhortations to the religious life than a structured pattern of day to day living. It was therefore flexible and easily adapted to particular needs. However, Dominic had also been drawn to the Norbertine Rule, which was based on the Augustinian Rule but with greater structure, and he skilfully combined the two to make a Rule uniquely adapted to the Dominican charism. Its flexibility meant that the Dominican Order has been able to engage in a wide variety of apostolates over the centuries, able to meet new challenges with creativity and vision.

A Rule of Love

The adoption of the Augustinian Rule was not just a question of expediency. It arose from Dominic's deep assimilation of its specific orientation, which could be summed up in its opening sentence: 'Before all else, dear brothers, love God and then your neighbour, because these are the chief commandments given to us.' No. 2 adds, 'The main purpose for you having come together is to live harmoniously in your house, intent upon God in oneness of mind and heart.'

There could not have been a statement of intent that went more to the heart of Dominic's vision for his Order and one that at the same time challenged the Cathar/Gnostic belief system. It is strange that while there was an orientation towards the 'good God' in Catharism, there is a strange lack of genuine love in their beliefs. The wisdom 'gnosis', to which they aspired was not an awakening into the nature of God, which is love, but an initiation into an esoteric belief system of gods and demi-gods, inherited from the Gnostics, although it is not certain how much of this was adopted by the Cathars. In any case, by rejecting belief in Jesus as the Son of God, seeing him as only a created angel, they were unable to understand the nature of God, for love, which is God's very essence and being, can only be given and received; love given and received in the 'wonderful exchange' between the Father and the Son, which is the Holy Spirit. They could not understand the true nature of love, because they rejected the ultimate expression of love which was the sacrifice and death of Jesus on the Cross, the ultimate expression of the utter love of Father and Son, poured out in the Holy Spirit, given for love of the human being that was their supreme creation.

In rejecting the Most Blessed Trinity, they were also rejecting their own humanity, of which their rejection of marriage was one symbol, and which death by starvation or poison was the most extreme manifestation. By contrast, the Catholic, Scriptural faith, sees marriage between a man and a woman as the earthly embodiment of the love of Christ for his Church; this again is a reflection of the love shared within the Trinity and therefore holy.

Because Dominic saw the nature of his Order as being built on love, love of God, manifested in the mutual love between the brethren, and which had to flow out to the souls they served, he was able to imbue his Order with the true 'gnosis', the true wisdom, of sacrificial love. This is a wisdom, the heart knowledge of which the Scriptures speak, that cannot be attained by our own efforts, as the Cathars strove to attain for their own version of 'gnosis'. It is the pure gift of God, given freely, but given most freely of all to the humble of heart. We can only prepare ourselves to receive what God wants to give.

The Charism of Preaching

All religious orders have the basics in common—the profession of poverty, chastity, obedience, to which another vow might be added, such as the Benedictine vow of hospitality. Within this framework, each Order has a distinct charism that emphasises one or other aspect of the religious life: Benedictines were bound to the recitation of the Divine Office, lived lives in common, following a life of prayer, asceticism and mutual charity, ordered round the singing of the Divine Office, with only limited time allotted to private prayer. Saint Teresa of Avila reversed this for her Carmelites, simplifying the recitation of the Divine

Office to give more time to mental prayer. Franciscans emphasise poverty.

Dominic saw that the specific charism of his Order would be the preaching of the Gospel, and so ordered the life of his friars to this end. The Divine Office, which was so dear to his heart, should be said '*breviter et succincte*', in other words, not with the solemn and elaborate ritual of the contemplative Orders that expressed the worship of the Church, so that more time could be given to study and preaching. In a novel move, dispensations from the Rule could be given to this end if necessary. Dominic loved poverty, and made sure that his houses and each friar showed forth evangelical poverty. However, he recognised that they could not live the extreme poverty that Saint Francis wanted for his friars, because they needed the books and the facilities indispensable to their vocation of study and preaching. And precious books needed to be housed where they could be kept safely.

There was another departure from traditional monasticism, and which arose from his work with the Cistercians. The great monastic orders were contemplative, often in isolated parts of the country. With the movement of people from the countryside into towns that marked this period, these Orders were becoming isolated from the people who needed their spiritual guidance. Dominic would therefore establish his houses where the people were, in towns and cities. Like his Master, Dominic when he 'saw the vast crowd, his heart was moved with pity for them, for they were like a sheep without a shepherd; and he began to teach them.' (Mark 6:34) He wanted to be wherever there were souls to be won.

St. Romain

The brothers returned to Toulouse, where Bishop Foulques gave them the custody of three churches, one in the village of Pamiers, one between Sorèze and Puylaurens and one in Toulouse, St. Romain. The first two the young community did not use for themselves but were given to the nuns to form the hub of convents. At St. Romain a humble cloister was built and the brothers moved into it in the summer of 1216, since Peter Seila's house was no longer large enough for them. St. Romain was small enough, with only the friars' cells, which had no doors to them, and a refectory. The cells themselves contained only a cane bedstead and a bench. Dominic intended that this house should provide the model for all future houses of the Order, and on his return from Rome he added two more rooms, one for meetings and another for holding their habits.

Return to Rome

With the community settled into their new home, Dominic made plans to return to Rome to seek papal approbation for their Order, when news reached them of the death of Pope Innocent 111 July 16. The new Pope, Honorius 111, was elected two days later. This was a severe blow to Dominic, because he could not be sure that the new Pope would be as sympathetic to his revolutionary Order as Innocent had been.

He set off for Rome, therefore, in some trepidation that autumn, but he need not have worried. The new Pope was just as enthusiastic for the reform of the Church as was his predecessor. The elderly Pope was a popular choice with the Romans, as he himself was a Roman, and he was loved for his kindness. During his pontificate he did all he could to win people over by peaceful means, rather than by confrontation, although he could be firm when the occasion needed it. However, when Dominic arrived in Rome he had some time to wait, because Honorius was away from the capital, and when he did arrive he had a great deal of business to deal with before he could grant an audience to Dominic. Dominic therefore spent his time praying, more often than not praying for hours on end in one or other of Rome's many churches, often huddled on the altar steps overnight in his patched habit, absorbed in prayer.

However, during Dominic's previous visit to Rome he had met one of the most influential men at the Papal Court, Cardinal Ugolino Conti, who hade been equally impressed by Dominic's manifest holiness and attractive personality. The Cardinal was also a dear and steadfast friend to Francis of Assisi, and he had already spoken to Pope Honorius about Dominic's new Order.

The ground had therefore already been prepared for Dominic, and there were no problems in granting him the approbation he sought. Honorius, too, was totally won over by this humble, radiant little monk, and was reluctant to let him return to Toulouse. He made him what was later titled 'Master of the Sacred Palace', the duties of which included being the Pope's theologian, teaching the Court and its Cardinals, and censoring books presented for approval. Dominicans have filled the post ever since.

Dominic finally obtained the Papal Bulls 22 December 1216. The first Bull confirmed Bishop Foulques' approbation, and all the gifts of land, revenues and churches. It showed how well the Pope had understood the special charism of the Order:

> Honorius, bishop, servant of the servants of
> God, to our dear son Dominic, prior of St.
> Romaine at Toulouse, and to your brethren
> who have made or will make profession of
> regular life, health and apostolic benediction.
> We, considering that the brethren of the
> Order will be the champions of the faith and
> true lights of the world, do confirm the Order
> in all its lands and possessions present and to
> come and we take under our protection and
> government the Order itself, with all its goods
> and rights.

The third Bull, given 26 January 1217, gives the Order
the title first given by Innocent, and which ever after
proudly designates it—Preachers. A friend of Cardinal
Ugolino met Dominic at the Cardinal's home and gave
a touching tribute to him: 'We spoke to together many
times of the eternal salvation of our own souls and those of
all men. I have met many holy, religious men and women,
but I never spoken to a man of equal perfection, or one
so taken up by the things of God.' William wanted to
join Dominic's Order, so it was agreed that, since he first
needed to deepen his studies in Theology at the University
of Paris, he would then rejoin Dominic in his mission
in the east. It is not surprising that Dominic influenced
many others to join him.

Vision of his Mission

Dominic spent much of his time praying in its Churches,
and there received a vision of Saints Peter and Paul in

which Peter gave him a staff and Paul gave him a book, and bade him go and preach, because this is the work for which God had designed him. In the vision he saw his sons stepping out two by two throughout the world. This vision perhaps explained a step that Dominic took on his return to Toulouse in May, and which met with opposition from the brethren at first.

He gathered the brothers and told them that he intended to send them on missions to all the countries where they were needed. In normal circumstances this would have been a very risky venture. His Order was young and they were only just beginning to establish themselves. They surely needed to be more grounded in the discipline and customs of the religious life. Most of the members were young, and many thought that it was risky to send such young and good-looking friars, so romantic in their patched habits and joyful zeal, to labour without the companionship of older and wiser brothers to guide them. Dominic was not deterred. He trusted his 'boys' as they were called, and they in turn responded joyfully to his leadership, that was marked by his own joy in living a faith-filled life, his evenness of temper and his willingness to entrust responsibility to them even at a young age. He set high standards of austerity and self-denial, but none so high as his own, and they willingly rose to the challenge.

Dominic usually accepted the judgment of others, but now he remained firm, saying: 'don't oppose me. I know very well what I'm doing. The seed will moulder if it is hoarded up. It will bear fruit if it is sown.' He knew his boys better than any, and, even more, he had absolute trust in the providence of God.

The criticism that Dominic received endured. His successor, Jordan of Saxony, as Master of the Order, had the same problem but also the same confidence in God's guidance and the same response. At one point Jordan received sixty young men into the Order in Paris, most of them uneducated, scarcely able to read the lessons at Matins. He was challenged fiercely about this policy at a General Chapter, but was as undeterred as Dominic had been. 'Let them be,' he replied. Do not despise one of these little ones. I tell you that you will see many of them, nearly all of them, in fact, turn out to be splendid preachers, through whom the Lord will work more for the salvation of soul than he does through many more intelligent and educated men.' His prophecy turned out to be true. Unsurprising, because Jordan, like Dominic, knew his Scriptures, and knew that the Lord had a predilection for using the weak ones of the world, what is foolish in the eyes of the world, to shame the strong, as Saint Paul put it.

Dominic must also have had in mind the vision of Saints Peter and Paul and his friars going out into the world to preach the Gospel. In his talks with William of Monserrat at the home of Cardinal Ugolino, he had come to realise that in the Languedoc he was more a defender of the faith against those who opposed it than a preacher of the Gospel. Now, he wanted to extend his ministry and that of his brothers to proclaiming the Gospel, to deepening the faith of believers, and bringing it, in addition, to those who had never heard it before. This had profound repercussions for the future of the Order. Dominic loved discussions and debates—and Dominicans ever since have followed in his footsteps!—but preaching cannot be confined to the unconverted. By extending his ministry to all, believers and unbelievers alike, Dominic also extended the scope of his Order, to give them the freedom and flexibility to preach wherever they were, in whatever form was most appropriate.

There was another reason that Dominic did not confide to his brethren, and that was that he had received a vision in which he was forewarned of the death of Simon de Montfort, the return of Count Raymond and the reversal of fortunes for the Catholics. Aware of the persecution and turmoil to come, he realised that his main mission to Cathar territory had gone as far as it could for the present. Just as Jesus had warned his followers of the fall of Jerusalem and they were then able to flee before catastrophe happened, so Dominic would disperse his followers, with the same beneficial effect—that just as the first Christians had been dispersed to the four corners of the world and thus were given a providential opportunity to spread the Gospel, so he would send out his friars from Toulouse, so that the dispersal of the first Dominicans would spread the Order throughout the world.

Some brothers felt that they were not sufficiently ready to be sent out into unknown fields. Dominic wanted Brother Peter Sella to go to Limoges, but he protested his ignorance and lack of books to help him in his studies, as he had only the homilies of Gregory the Great. 'Go with confidence, my son,' Dominic replied. Twice a day I will present you before God. Have no doubts, you will win many people for God and bear much fruit.' Another prophecy that came true, for Peter died there, full of honour in the fullness of age

John of Spain testified that 'he had such confidence in God's goodness that he sent even ignorant men to preaching, saying "Do not be afraid, the Lord will be with you and will put power in your mouths"'.

The brothers, as they went out, were heartened by the fact that they knew they were supported by the prayers of a saint and Dominic's confidence in them. Dominic trusted his friars, he prayed unceasingly for them, and knew that, above all, they had the grace of the Holy Spirit to inspire them. It is little wonder that so many grew to the stature of which Dominic, and God, knew they were capable.

A Sorrowful Sermon

On the day of the dispersal the brethren gathered at Prouille on the Feast of the Assumption 1217, so that the nuns could also be included in this gathering, as Dominic put the undertaking under the protection of Our Lady. People arrived from Toulouse, joining the townsfolk of Prouille; some Cistercians came, and Simon de Montfort with his family attended. Dominic sang the Mass and preached the sermon, the content of which surprised the gathered congregation. In the Gospels, Jesus had many radiant words of encouragement, comfort and love to speak to those who sought him, but he could also be stern and challenging. The townsfolk had been used to Dominic encouraging them, speaking words of joy and hope, but now he spoke with the sternness of Christ himself. It is easy enough to listen to comforting words and sermons, but they should challenge, too, a challenge the people of Toulouse had failed to heed. He could also discern that there was simmering unrest in the city which, before he left in September, would boil over into revolt, riots and mayhem.

Simon had returned after a triumphant visit to King Philip of France, celebrating his victories, although a recent attempt to lift the siege of Beaucaire had ended in failure. During his absence Count Raymond had won back the people to his side; although Simon de Montfort had brought a semblance of peace to the city he had never won over the hearts of the people; now they were ready to rise up against him. So it was with great sadness that Dominic addressed the people: 'For many years now I have sung to you gently by preaching, imploring and weeping,' he said to them. 'But, as it is commonly said in my country, "Where blessing is of no avail, the stick should prevail." So we shall call out against you princes and prelates who, unfortunately, will convoke against this territory peoples and kingdoms and will kill many by the edge of the sword, will destroy towers, cast down and demolish walls and reduce all of you, alas, into slavery. In this way, the stick, that is, the strength of the stick, will prevail, where blessing and sweetness was of no avail.'

Just as Jesus wept over Jerusalem and foresaw its destruction, now, Dominic likewise wept over his adopted city, seeing its downfall. He would have to leave them, and he would leave them with the sorrow of failure.

Dispersal

After addressing the people, Dominic then spoke to his assembled brothers, reminding them of their mission, encouraging them to have confidence and courage as they would set out bearing their message of peace and truth. They then made their vows in Dominic's hands. The nuns of Prouille also then pronounced their vows.

Departure to the Mission Field

It was time for the small group to disperse on their mission, and Dominic assigned them their work. William Claret and Brother Noel would stay behind at Prouille to minister to the sisters, and Peter Seila and Thomas would stay at St. Romain. Brothers Michael of Uzero, Dominic the Little, Peter of Madrid and Sueiro Gómez would go to Spain and Portugal. Matthew of France, Bertrand of Garrigua, Michael of Fabra, Oderic, Dominic's brother Mannes, John of Navarre and Lawrence the Englishman would go to the University of Paris, because Dominic intended his friars to have bases in all the University cities of Europe, where they could train future members of the Order. Stephen of Metz Dominic kept for his own companion.

Perhaps remembering the example of Francis of Assisi, Dominic made one stipulation that they should go out 'without scrip or purse.' This so shocked the Cistercians when they heard of it that they accused Dominic for sending out 'unlettered boys'. 'I am certain that these boys of mine will go and return safely,' Dominic replied. Only the novice, John of Navarre insisted that he needed a little money for travelling expenses, and out of compassion for his youth, although with sadness for his lack of trust, Dominic gave him twelve pence. Like his Master, Dominic would not crush the bruised reed, but gave his brothers the freedom to develop and grow into the fullness of their potential.

Finally, he insisted that the brothers should elect an abbot who could take over the leadership of the Order— Dominic cherished the desire to go to Tartary (as the lands of Central Asia, east of the Caspian Sea were known) and hopefully be martyred there; he had already begun to grow a beard in order to fit in more easily. They chose Matthew of France, an older man, a holy priest and revered for his wisdom and practical experience. He had been Prior of the church of St Vincent in Castres before joining the Friars Preachers. An incident concerning him took place when Dominic visited the Castres priory one day and celebrated Mass in the church there, that might have inspired Matthew to join the Dominicans. Dominic remained behind after Mass to pray, and when a brother was sent to call him to the refectory as the meal was ready, found the saint raised nine inches above the ground in ecstasy. He ran back to tell his prior of the phenomenon who saw it with his own eyes, but Dominic was now raised eighteen inches above the ground. They stayed there until Dominic literally came down to earth and lay prostrate, as was his custom, before the altar.

Matthew was also to be the first and last Abbot of the Order, because at the General Chapter of 1220 the title was abolished in favour of the designation of Master, while heads of convents were known as priors. Dominic handed over to him the Bull of Confirmation, and then they were ready to set out.

Journey to Rome

Dominic needed papal approval to go to Tartary, so in October he and Stephen of Metz set off on foot for Rome, although others joined them *en route*. He was a good companion to have on a journey that demanded courage and a willingness to suffer the hardships of such a journey. Walking barefoot, when their feet were cut and bruised by the sharp stones or drenched with rain, he would turn to them with his characteristic cheerfulness and genuine joy, exclaiming, 'this is penance!' How could anyone hold back, then, given such an example! To urge them on their way he would lead them in the singing of hymns such as the *Ave Maris Stella* and *Veni Creator Spiritus*. As they approached a town or village he would stop and pray, weeping, for the people who lived there, a living reminder that they were there to save souls, to bring them closer to God. Sometimes he would be so lost in prayer that his companions would lose sight of him, and they would have retrace their steps, only to find him kneeling, wrapped in contemplation, oblivious of any of the dangers from wild animals or bandits around him. Such awareness of the depths of his prayer and union with Christ made them acutely aware, when they were with him, of the presence of God in their midst. His companions testified that wherever they were, his conversation was always of God or with God.

Although Dominic was of but middle height and build he possessed a strong constitution, and he asked of himself greater austerity than he ever asked of others. He himself always fasted on his journeys, and when they arrived at a convent or monastery to ask for shelter, he would always join in the Divine Office, however tired he was, and preach to the community. Even then, he would remain in church overnight, praying, although fatigue would sometimes overcome him; he would sometimes drop off to sleep in the middle of his frugal meal. He never had a cell or room of his own.

At every town and village through which they passed they would stop and preach. Dominic would walk barefoot, then put on his shoes before entering the town.

On one occasion a young man asked him what books he studied, so impressed was he by the depth of Dominic's understanding and knowledge of the Scriptures. 'I have studied in the book of charity more than any other, my son,' he replied. 'It is the book that teaches us everything.'

CHAPTER 6

ROME

Dominic received a warm welcome from Pope Honorius 111 on his arrival in Rome early in February 1218, who gave him a Bull that gave him entry into all dioceses to preach and minister the sacraments. He also gave Dominic the church of St. Sixtus on the Appian Way. This was in a state of disrepair, because Honorius had intended it to house a community of Guilbertine nuns, and draw together nuns from other orders to form a single community, but the plans had come to nothing. The church was in a deserted street that had in ancient times been the Patrician quarter of the city. Undeterred, Dominic accepted the gift and set in train the necessary renovations, lodging in the meantime in an almshouse near the Lateran. That the new foundation, the cradle of the Dominican Order in Rome, was blessed by God, was attested by the miracles that took place. During the repairs, a mason was excavating under a part of the building when it collapsed on top of him. The brothers ran to the spot but thought they were too late to save him, buried as he was under a mass of rubble. Dominic ordered them to dig the man out while he prayed, and he was brought out alive and unharmed.

Raising a Child to Life

Another time, a Roman widow, Guatonia, attended a sermon Dominic was preaching in the Church of St. Mark; she came home to find that her only son, who was sick, had died while she was out. Accompanied by her servants, she brought the lifeless body of her son to Dominic, laying him at the saint's feet, begging his prayers. Moved with compassion, Dominic prayed for the child, who was restored to life. Dominic charged the mother not to say anything about the miracle, but of course she did. Soon, all Rome had heard of it, including the Pope, who ordered it to be announced from all the pulpits in Rome. Deeply distressed, Dominic begged him to countermand the order, saying that otherwise he would be obliged to leave Rome and go to preach to the Saracens. The Pope was deaf to his pleas, though; Dominic was already drawing great crowds to his sermons in St. Mark's and now Dominic found himself the centre of an enthusiastic crowd wherever he went, eager to touch him, cutting off pieces of his habit to keep as relics of a saint in their midst. He was reduced to looking almost like a scarecrow. In the end, Dominic gave in gracefully, even stopping his brothers when they tried to keep the crowd away from him, saying 'Let them alone; we have no right to hinder their devotion.' Like many a saint before him, he was able to detach himself from the adulation, recognising that God was using him as a means of grace to others; that in the words of Saint Paul, he was profoundly aware that he was only an earthen vessel into which God's grace was poured.

As well as his indefatigable preaching, Dominic was aware of the needs of individuals, especially women recluses who lived near the basilicas, immured in the

Aurelian walls in the utmost degradation, their spiritual needs ignored. He gave them talks, heard their confessions and cured their illnesses. One, Sister Bona, who lived by herself in a tower by the Lateran Gate he cured of a hideous breast cancer. Sister Lucy, who lived behind the church of Saint Anastasia, he cured of an affliction that had stripped her arm of flesh from her shoulder to her hand.

The Miracle of Bread

Another miracle benefited his own brothers. Twice he provided miraculously for them when their food ran out. Men flocked to join the new Order, and one day, when their numbers had swollen to about a hundred, Dominic commanded Brother John of Calabria and Brother Albert of Rome to go into the city and beg for alms. They begged all day without success, and were returning home when, by the church of St. Anastasia, they met a woman who had great esteem for the Order. She gave them a loaf of bread, saying that she would not want them to go back quite empty-handed. A little further on, they met a man who begged them for alms. At first they protested that they had nothing, but under his begging they said, 'What can we do with only one loaf? Let us give it to him for the love of God.' The man left them, and when they returned home Dominic met them, having been made aware by the Holy Spirit of what had transpired, and said cheerfully, 'Children, have you nothing?' The brothers told him what had happened, but he replied, 'It was an angel of the Lord: the Lord will know how to provide for his own; let us go and pray.'

Dominic went into the church to pray and then summoned to the refectory the brothers who were understandably reluctant to obey, as they knew there was nothing to eat. However, in the end they obeyed, and as Brother Henry the Roman began to read, as is the custom during meal times, Dominic prayed and two beautiful young men came in bearing loaves in white cloths hung from their shoulders. They began distributing the bread, which had an admirable beauty. Then they needed wine, but everyone knew there was none left. Nevertheless, Dominic told the servers, 'Go to the vessel and pour out to the brethren the wine which the Lord has sent them.' They found the vessel full to the brim, and the brethren had more food and drink than they had had for some time. The supplies lasted three days, and after that what remained was given to the poor.

Our Lady's Protection of the Order

From the very beginning, when Dominic received the vision at Prouille, Our Lady showed her special predeliction for the Order. Brother Lawrence the Englishman, when the Paris foundation was going through much hardship, received a vision of Our Lady in which he encouraged them to persevere. In Rome, Dominic also received a vision for the whole Order. He had stayed praying in the church until midnight and then had come up to the dormitory where he remained standing in prayer. He suddenly became rapt in spirit before God, as Sister Cecilia, who recorded the episode, put it, when he saw Our Lord and the Blessed Virgin sitting on the right side of the Father. 'It seemed to

Dominic that Our Lady was wearing a cape of bright blue, the colour of sapphire. As he looked around, Dominic could see religious of all other Orders but his around the throne. He began to weep bitterly and stood afar off, not daring to approach the Lord and His Mother. Then Our Lady motioned him to come near, but he did not dare to do so until Our Lord also called him. He was still weeping bitterly until Our Lord told him to rise and asked him the cause of his tears. 'I am weeping because I see all the other Orders but no sign of my own,' Dominic replied. 'Do you want to see your Order?' the Lord asked, then putting his hand on the shoulders of the Blessed Virgin He said to Dominic, 'I have entrusted your Order to My Mother. Do you want to see your Order?' Our Lady then opened the cape which covered her and spread it out before Blessed Dominic, to whom it seemed vast enough to cover the entire heaven and, under it, he saw a large multitude of the brethren.' The bell then rang for Matins, and Dominic came to himself.

News from his Other Foundations

While such marvels were happening, Dominic kept in contact with his friars scattered around the various countries. He heard news from Spain that Gomez and Peter were having great success in the Spanish mission, and a copy of the Bull was sent to the Spanish bishops so that the friars would have no hindrance in preaching the Gospel throughout Spain. Michael of Uzero and Dominic of Segovia had less success, though, partly because of the local bishops' suspicion of this new and seemingly unorthodox Order. They returned to join Dominic in

Rome, humiliated and depressed that they had failed in their mission. To restore their lost confidence and as an assurance of his faith in them, Dominic lost no time in sending them to the university city of Bologna to make a new foundation; apart from this consideration for the brothers, he was also determined to increase the number of houses of study for his friars.

The Paris Foundation

The brothers in Paris were having a hard time, too. Even though the brothers were poorly housed near Notre Dame and the school of theology—its one advantage—they found themselves unwelcome by the well-established clergy, who considered their begging as almost akin to heresy, and who did not want instruction from these disreputable friars. The other Orders established in the town were also incensed that young men were flocking to this upstart order. However, hearing that the brothers at the University of Paris were not well housed, the Pope himself sent an urgent letter to the authorities asking them to provide better accommodation for them, and they were soon settled in a new building in the Rue Saint-Jacques.

Another problem was that the established Orders were afraid that this new Order would deprive them of houses, revenues and resources, a problem that affected their foundations in other towns and cities. Once the Paris foundation was established, Bertrand and John came to Rome to discuss the problems and how they solved them, and Dominic sent them to Bologna so that their experience could help that foundation, too.

Master Reginald Joins the Order

Even greater help was on its way to the Bologna foundation. Reginald, dean of the church of Orleans, was accompanying his bishop on a pilgrimage to the Holy Land, and they stopped for a while in Rome. Still a young man, Reginald had a brilliant intellect and was a world-renowned canonist, holding the chair of Canon Law at the University of Paris. However, there was an unsatisfied longing within him that fame could not satisfy. He longed to abandon all his worldly acclaim for a way of life of poverty and a share in the Cross of Christ in which he could devote himself to the salvation of souls. He hoped that in the Holy Land he would receive some answer to what form of vocation he should follow. At this point he met Cardinal Ugolino and the young man discussed his problems with him. Ugolino sent him to Dominic, and the two men immediately knew that they were kindred souls; Reginald understood, too, that the Order of Friars Preachers was the answer to his prayers.

Before he could don the habit, though, he was struck down by one of the deadly fevers that plagued Rome. Dominic was deeply grieved at the thought of losing such a promising son and pleaded with God for his life, even it if were for just a short time. While he was praying Reginald, burning with fever, received a vision of Our Lady, accompanied by young maidens, in which she addressed him, saying, 'Ask of me what you will, and I will give it to you.' One of the maidens suggested that Reginald should ask for nothing, but simply that he should leave everything to the will and pleasure of the Queen of Mercy, to which the Blessed Humbold, who chronicled the incident added, 'to the which he right willingly assented.' Then the Mother of God anointed his hands, feet, nostrils, mouth and eyes, saying a prayer for each of his senses, with a prayer for chastity, and that his feet would be shod for the preaching of the Gospel of Peace. She then showed him the habit of the Friars Preachers, saying, 'Behold the habit of your Order', and then disappeared, leaving Reginald restored to complete health.

Dominic visited him the following morning and Reginald told him of the vision, and especially about the habit that was shown to him. This included a white scapular. Until now, the brothers had worn the habit of the Canons Regular of St. Augustine, but the linen rochet had already proved itself unsuitable for the long and dusty journeys undertaken by the brothers. Dominic decided that they should change the habit to the white scapular revealed in the vision, and Reginald begged him not to mention his part in the change until after his death, which he had been given to understand would not be long in coming.

The Dominican Habit

The habit was of profound significance to Dominic; when he gave the brothers the habit, he promised them 'the bread of life and the water of heaven.' Those thus clothed would be assured that, as they pursued their religious life, the habit would be their 'bread of life', that they would always have the basic necessities they would need to sustain them in their calling; the staff of life, as bread is called, and the 'water of heaven', the refreshment, the 'light yoke' that would give them joy in their apostolate.

Reginald, clothed now in the Dominican habit, with his bishop, continued his journey to the Holy Land.

By now Dominic was eager to visit his sons in their various foundations, and with his Roman houses prospering and stable it was time for him to do so. In October of 1218 he therefore set out for Bologna.

CHAPTER 7

TRAVELS

Dominic had sent John of Navarre and later Brother Christian and a lay brother Peter to Bologna early in 1218 to make the foundation. Also there were Michael of Ucero and Dominic of Segovia, after their fruitless mission in Spain. When Dominic arrived at Bologna he found the five brothers living in great poverty and difficulty, yet following the Rule with the utmost faithfulness and perfection. As yet, no-one had joined them to swell their numbers. They had been given two houses attached to a church called Santa Maria della Mascarella, but the accommodation was so small that it was barely enough for the five friars. Their cells measured only four foot by seven foot, just enough to hold a narrow bed and the barest of other necessities.

The five brothers welcomed Dominic with great joy, but it was soon apparent that they were deeply despondent at their lack of success in the city and the hardships of their extreme poverty. Dominic gently encouraged them to persevere, and was able to give them further encouragement by telling them of the marvellous events surrounding Reginald's admittance into the Order, and the glad news that Reginald would be joining them shortly, on his return from the Holy Land. He stayed with them for only a short while, as he was anxious to go on to Spain and the struggling foundation there. He sent Friars John of Navarre and Bertrand of Garrigua back to Paris, Friar John continued to study at the University. Bertrand he arranged would act as a liaison between Dominic and the various communities. Only Friar Christian and Brother Peter were left to welcome Reginald when he arrived on the 21st December. Dominic and his party had already left for Spain by then, and it is likely that he took with him Dominic of Segovia and Michael of Ucero, both Spaniards.

Reginald's arrival meant a complete reversal of the fortunes of the Bologna foundation. Within a week, his vibrant and dynamic preaching had galvanised the city, and people flocked to listen to him. The little church of Santa Maria della Mascarella soon proved too small to hold those who came, and he had to preach in the squares and streets. Where people listened, men young and old flocked into the Order, some of the most eminent of their time.

Roland of Cremona

One of the first to seek admittance to the Order was Roland of Cremona, the public lecturer at the University. Perhaps because their way of life was such a reproach to the other religious orders, the original friars met with great opposition and persecution, so much so that some of them were so discouraged that they were ready to give up, not yet having seen the fruits of Reginald's preaching They were gathered in chapter discussing the situation when the door opened and Roland came in humbly begging to be clothed in the habit. Reginald took the scapular from his own shoulders and flung it over Roland's; this was the encouragement and the affirmation from the Lord that they needed, that such an eminent man would seek to join them, and there was no more talk of giving up.

Master Moneta

Students, some of the most promising from the university, were not long in joining Roland, and their exodus into this unknown and untried Order was causing one of the professors, Master Moneta, great concern and not a little annoyance and frustration. His students eventually dared him to go to one of Reginald's sermons, and he reluctantly agreed, although he said that he wanted to go to Mass first. He heard three Masses until he ran out of excuses and reluctantly made his way to the church; he had left it so late that there was no more room inside the church, and he stood awkwardly in the doorway, hoping to be invisible. Reginald was preaching on the saint of the day, Saint Stephen:

'Behold I see the heaven open, and Jesus standing at the right hand of God. Heaven is open today also; the door is always open to him who is willing to enter. Why do you delay? Why do you linger on the threshold? What blindness, what negligence is this? The heavens are still open!'

Master Moneta no longer lingered on the threshold and waylaid Reginald as he came down from the pulpit, begging to be received into the Order. He served a year's probation and then was allowed to enter, inspiring even more of his students to follow his example, and bringing even more prestige and acceptance to the fledgling Order.

Move to St Nicholas of the Vineyards

Within six months an estimated one hundred men, mainly professors and students, had donned the Dominican habit, and the advice went round that it would be well for the unconvinced to avoid Friar Reginald's sermons lest the same outcome should happen to them. Santa Maria della Mascarella soon became too small to hold them all, and in the early Spring of 1219 they moved just outside the city walls to the church and convent of St. Nicholas of the Vineyards. Legends had already surrounded the property, because workers in the vineyard had heard angels singing, and the conviction was that that one day it would be a place of pilgrimage and prayer. The property was given them, somewhat reluctantly, by the wealthy d'Andaló family, at the pleading of their daughter, Diana, who had been drawn to the Dominicans after hearing the sermons of Master Raymond.

Once the Bologna foundation had become established a papal legate, Conrad, bishop of Porto arrived, somewhat in two minds about this new Order, so different from any other. What purpose did it serve in the life of the Church. Was it from man or from God? As he sat in church surrounded by the brothers he asked for a book and a Missal was brought to him. Making the sign of the cross over it he opened the pages and his eyes lighted on the words, 'Laudare, benedicere et praedicare.'—praise, bless, preach. This convinced him that this new movement was indeed of God, and assured the brothers, 'Although I wear the external habit of another profession, I wear yours internally about my soul. Be assured that I am entirely yours. I am of your Order, and I commend myself to you with all my affection.'

The life of the Bologna brothers has been described by the early chronicler as 'so wonderful was their regular observance and their continual and fervent prayer; so extraordinary their poverty in eating, in their beds and clothes, and all such things, that never had been the like seen before in the city.'

Journey to Spain

Meanwhile, Dominic was making his way to Spain, with a growing band of friars who joined him on the way. With Dominic and his party of friars was a Franciscan, and as they were leaving Bologna for Spain a fierce dog jumped out at them and mauled the Franciscan's habit so badly that was impossible for him to continue the journey. Dominic took some mud and smeared it over the rents in the habit, and when the mud was washed off, to the amazement of all, the robe was perfectly restored.

He set out with only a staff in his hand and a book of Saint Matthew's Gospel near his heart. These were not mere symbols but expressions of the deep reality of his inner life and his personification of all that his Order stood for; it was to be a mendicant, travelling, preaching Order, and the message the friars bore was the Gospel of Christ, which should be in their minds and their heart.

Dominic's visitations to the various foundations were not a mere bureaucratic necessity but an expression of the bond that united his Order. Friars Preachers: friars, which meant they were wandering beggars for the love of Christ, traversing countries to be where people were to give them the Gospel, the Good News, of Christ. They were bidden to meditate on that Gospel, not only in the silence and seclusion of their cells, but as they travelled, talking about the Gospel, discussing disputing, but above all praying, so that the words of Scripture, learned by heart, should permeate their whole discourse. In a sense, the open road, the streets and squares, the halls of study and parish churches are the Dominican's monastery. There was even a concrete expression of that in the early houses, where there were no doors to the cells, reminding the friars that their studies in which they engaged in their cells, was to prepare them to go out and share with the world, that their studies could not be divorced from the world outside.

Ever since Dominic's days the Master would visit the Order's houses throughout the world, the visible symbol of their united apostolate, however far-flung the houses, and however diverse the ways in which they expressed that apostolate.

Meditating on the Scriptures

Their houses were vital to maintain their brotherly life together, but at the first Bologna Chapter that Dominic would shortly convene, he urged the novices to take their studies with them, whether they were in their cell or on the road, 'how they should be intent on study, so that by day and by night, at home or on a journey, they should be reading or reflecting on something; whatever they can, they should try to commit to memory.' Dominic himself reflected so long on the Scriptures that he knew them virtually by heart. As Saint Catherine of Siena, the lay Dominican of the Third Order said later, they should take their inner cell, the cell of their heart, with them, so that at any time they could retire within it to commune with God.

How well this was observed can be seen in the extant letters of Jordan of Saxony. To give just one example; he writes to Diana d'Andaló:

> For the rest, beloved, be strengthened in the Lord and in the might of his power, and give strength to your sisters; and rejoice continually in him in whose right hand are joys that endure for ever. For soon now the time will come for the wedding-feast of the Lamb whose right hand is filled with gifts to console those who weep with longing for their true country and to give drink to those whose souls are bitter with the thirst of love; he will wipe away the tearful waters of this present time, and turn their sad insipidity into the wine of the saints, the noble wine which rejoices the heart of man and inebriates with sweetness the beloved of God, the wine of everlasting gladness, the splendid new wine which at the banqueting-table of the court of heaven is poured out for his chosen ones by the Son of God who is blessed for ever and ever.

In just this one paragraph there are nine direct Scripture references, but even more the whole of the passage is saturated with scriptural imagery and inferences. Jordan had imbibed the Scriptures so well that they became his own language.

Prayer and Study

As is often the case, a conflict can arise between prayer and study. A brother came to Master Jordan one day with just this dilemma: was it more useful for him to devote himself to his prayers or apply himself to studying the Bible? 'Which is better, to spend your whole time drinking, or to spend your whole time eating?' Jordan replied. 'Surely it is best for them to take their turn, and so it is, too in the other case.' Prayer, without listening to God speaking to us in the Scriptures can be dry and barren; studying the Scriptures without the watering and depth of prayer could likewise be barren. They are the two indispensable handmaids to growing in holiness and efficacy in preaching and sharing the Word of God. Saint Albert described study as 'the sweetness of seeking truth together', and this surely is an insight that is at the root of the Dominican charism, and its simple motto: Truth, Veritas.

The Grace of Preaching

Prayer and study for the Dominican was the handmaid of what they delightfully call the 'grace of preaching'. As well as being the means of their own understanding their faith and growth in holiness, they had to pass on the fruits of their prayer and study to others. Again, the art, the grace of preaching, had to be learnt and as with the balance between prayer and study, there were pitfalls. Humbert of Romans who became Master of the Order, was much exercised with the 'problem', and gave valuable advice that could apply to all who wish to pass on the faith, whether by preaching or by informal talks and discussion. First of all, he says, there are few good preachers, but likewise 'in the primitive Church there were few preachers, but they were so good they converted the whole world'. Many struggle to pass on the faith without succeeding, and the reason is that there is only One who can teach the art, and that is the Holy Spirit. It is God's gift, but the preacher has to co-operate to receive the gift. Art can degenerate into artifice and mere cleverness, and Humbert gives the amusing example of one man who gave as his text for a sermon on Saints Peter and Paul Numbers 3:20—'The sons of Meran were Moholi and Musi'. Humbert remarked that such twisting of the sense of the text is more likely to cause people to laugh at such a sermon than to draw benefit from it. But at least it shows Dominicans know their Bible!

So, Humbert says, 'since human effort can achieve nothing without the help of God, the most important thing of all for a preacher is that he should have recourse to prayer, asking God, to grant him speech that will be effective in bringing salvation to his hearers'.

Miracles on the Way to Spain

On their journeys the friars observed as well as they could the monastic framework of their day, praying the Office together, keeping the periods of silence and prayer. When they stayed in a convent Dominic would ask to preach to the community, and he would always attend Matins, the Night Office, however tired he was, staying to pray in the church afterwards, even though fatigue would some times overtake him. They spoke of God to any who would listen. At one point they met up with a saintly religious whose language they did not know but longed to converse with him; Dominic prayed, and obtained from the Lord the favour that each be able to speak the other's language. So they went on together for three days, able to understand each other.

A similar phenomenon took place on the journey from Toulouse to Paris. They arrived at the famous shrine that contained a miraculous statue of Our Lady of Rocamadour and which according to legend was the resting place of Zaccheus, the tax collector who entertained Jesus in his own home. Dominic and his travelling companion Bertrand spent the night in vigil at the church dedicated to her. The following day they continued their journey and met up with some German pilgrims who were reciting prayers and litanies to encourage them on their way. The German pilgrims invited the Dominicans to join them in what Blessed Jordan described as their 'customary hearty meal', and four days into their journey Dominic said to Brother Bernard that he would love to repay the Germans' generosity by giving them spiritual food, but could not, because he did not speak German. 'If you agree,' he said to Bernard, 'let us kneel down and ask the Lord to enable us to understand and speak their language so that we can speak to them of the Lord Jesus Christ.'

Then, to the amazement of the pilgrims, he was able to speak to them in their own language and was able to speak of God to them until they had to part and go their separate ways.

The journey was full of events. One day the party was caught in a downpour of rain, but Dominic made the sign of the cross and calmly kept on walking. All of them came through the storm untouched by the downpour. Another rainy day, they arrived at an inn and everyone tried to dry their clothes before the fire. Dominic went to the nearby church in his soaking clothes and spent the night in prayer. In the morning his clothes were completely dry while those of his party were still damp.

As they passed through the Lombard Alps, one of the Spanish brothers was so overcome with hunger and fatigue that he couldn't move another step. Dominic tried to encourage him without success, so he prayed, then told the brother go over to a certain rock. He found there a freshly baked loaf which renewed his strength, and Dominic told to him to put the remains back to where he had found it. It was not until they had started on their way again that the brother thought that it was a strange place to find a loaf of bread. Running to Dominic he asked who had put the bread there. 'Did you have enough to eat?' the saint replied. 'Yes' the brother said. 'Then give thanks to God and do not worry as to who had put it there.'

The Angelic Escort

In the city of Faenza Albert, the bishop, was so won over by Dominic's charm and eloquence that he invited him and a companion to stay at the palace. The servants told the bishop that Dominic always went to Matins in the nearby church of St. Andrew, even though all the doors were locked; they were at a loss to know how he did it so some of them stayed up and followed him, and reported that they had seen two handsome young men bearing lighted candles going before the two friars. Every door opened before them at a touch of a finger, the youths stayed during the singing of Matins, then escorted the Dominicans back to the bishop's palace. The bishop was so intrigued that he, too, stayed up to watch the phenomenon, and afterwards gave the church to the Order. To this day it is called the Angel's Field.

In Paris, Queen Blanche, mother of the French King Saint Louis, often invited Dominic to her court and he met there Alexander 11, King of Scotland, who was in the capital to arrange a royal marriage. The King asked him to send friars to Scotland, although it was another ten years before the Dominicans arrived there and set up several monasteries under the patronage of the King.

Toulouse

The party stopped at Toulouse, which was in turmoil following the death of Simon de Montfort. Some of the novices, perhaps due to the fatigue of the journey and the demands of the mendicant life, left Dominic at this point, although most returned later. Dominic was an indefatigable walker, only putting on his shoes when he entered the town, and it is estimated that he would walk between twenty five to thirty miles (forty to fifty kilometres) a day. If there was no religious house at the end of the day where they could stay, they would lodge in a hospice, which would invariably be infested with lice and fleas—nothing had changed, it seems some four hundred years later, when Saint Teresa of Avila described life as a night in a bad inn!

It is understandable that some of the brothers found it too difficult to endure. Sadly, Dominic, in the words of his Master, turning to the only three that remained and asked them, 'Will you also go away?' One of them replied for the others, too, 'God forbid that I should leave the head to follow the feet!' Poverty can seem romantic from the outside, but less easy to live out! Perhaps the novices were shocked and discouraged by the situation in Toulouse; to support and encourage the brothers there, Dominic left with them one of his most trusted friends, Bertrand of Garrigua, as superior, whose holiness and good sense would see the community through the trials that lay ahead.

Dominic and the remainder of his party went on to Fanjeaux and then Prouille to visit the friars and to hand over to them the bull of Honorius 111 that gave them canonical status, visiting the nuns also. He then crossed over the Pyrenees into Spain—in the depths of winter, so perhaps this, too, was too daunting a prospect for some of the brothers!—the first time he had set foot in his native land for sixteen years.

Segovia

He arrived at his homeland of Segovia just before Christmas, where he stayed for some weeks in order to set up a friary there. The brothers built it on the bank of the river and titled it the convent of the Holy Cross. Nearby was a grotto in the rock where Dominic would often spend his nights in prayer and penance. He possibly visited his relatives in the region, although it is possible that both his mother and father had died by then. Many of his nephews and nieces would enter his Order.

There had been a long drought in the country that had reduced the people to near starvation. One day, as Dominic preached to them he interrupted his sermon: 'Do not be afraid, brothers,' he reassured them, 'but trust in the divine mercy. I tell you good news. Today God will send you rain in plenty and the drought will be turned to plenty.' Even before he had finished his sermon the rain fell in such abundance that the people were drenched before they reached their homes. They had an abundant harvest that year, and the place of the miracle is marked by a small chapel.

He stayed in the house of a poor woman, but her neighbours all vied with her to try and spoil him, with very little success. There was Beceda and Nogueza, who testified at his canonization, complaining that they could not persuade him to eat more than a couple of eggs and a little porridge. Another one said that she tried in vain to make him sleep in a bed, but he insisted on sleeping on the floor and even throwing off the bed clothes. The woman would creep in and pull them back over him as he slept. All they could do was to provide him with a change of hair shirts, with the old ones kept jealously as relics of this humble and self-effacing saint in their midst. The woman with whom he lodged had reason to bless the hair shirt she kept as a prized possession, as she was sure its presence later on saved her house from burning down.

Madrid

From Segovia Dominic travelled to Madrid where he found the house too small for the friars. He moved them to a larger property, and established a community of nuns in the smaller house, placing his own brother Mannes there to look after them. He remained in Madrid until he was sure that the foundation was firmly established.

Foundations near the Universities

Dominic as wanted as many houses as possible, as near to Universities as possible; he wanted educated friars to spread the Gospel and give a good account of their faith to those who would oppose them, and also to those who wanted to deepen their own faith.

To begin with, the friars studied Scripture almost exclusively, but very soon their studies branched out from 'the Queen of Sciences', for nothing that is of the good, the true and the beautiful is alien to the Christian faith. This breadth of approach was personified in two towering figures, not only of the Dominican Order but of the Universal Church. Two years after the death of Dominic, Albert, eldest son of the Count of Bollstädt, won over by the preaching of Blessed Jordan of Saxony, who was now Dominic's successor as Master of the Order, entered the Dominican Order. He is known as Saint Albert the Great, great not only for his holiness but also for his learning that encompassed all that was known of the natural world in his day. He was the great naturalist of his day and nothing seemed to be outside the sphere of his curiosity, from a study of the moon, the stars, classifying with great precision minerals and plants. He also began spreading the ideas of Aristotle. In exploring the relationship between theology and secular science he recommended a strict separation between them, with each having its own methodology, while at the same time affirming that if they both approached a particular problem that concerned both, the results they arrived at would be in accord, since truth was one.

He was also the teacher of an even greater Dominican, Saint Thomas Aquinas. In his great works he diverged from his master by drawing up a synthesis between theology and scientific rationality, while affirming with Albert that the two were two aspects of the one truth. The science of nature and natural philosophy were ways towards truth, and Christian theology was an understanding of faith in the light of reason.

It is no accident that the Order should have produced two such towering and unique intellects, for it provided a milieu in which they could thrive and realise their potential to the full. Dominic had provided the flexibility to explore not only the Faith, but how the faith informed and embraced the world in which it found itself. It is ironic that the Middle Ages, the medieval world, is seen today as what represents, and provides the shorthand for, all that is the most oppressive and the most backward and superstitious in human development. Yet from a Catholic perspective it was the era that saw the rise of the universities that endure to the present, and two intellects that have perhaps never been surpassed. This was possible because the Catholic Faith provided the framework, the harmony between faith and reason, which allowed this to flourish. In the case of Albert the Great this was the union of faith and the science of his day. 'The aim of natural science is not simply to accept the statements of others, but to investigate the causes that are at work in nature,' he said. And this in an era that is caricatured as suppressing human investigation and independent thought!

He also said, 'In studying nature we have not to inquire how God the Creator may, as he freely wills, use His creatures to work miracles and thereby show forth His power: we have rather to inquire what Nature with its immanent causes can naturally bring to pass.' He did not deny miracles, but said that before ascribing something as a miracle it was necessary to look first for a natural explanation.

This was fully in line with the Scriptures: 'for God gave me sound knowledge of existing things, that I might know the organization of the universe and the force of its elements, the beginning and the end and the midpoint of times, the changes in the sun's course and the variations of the seasons, cycles of years, positions of the stars, natures of animals, tempers of beasts, powers of the winds and thoughts of men, uses of plants and virtues of roots. (Wisdom 7:7-20)

Harmony of Faith and Reason

The training given in the universities provided the tools that enabled the students to harmonise faith and reason, and the Middle Ages could in truth be titled the Age of Reason, as well as Faith. The students studied logic, reason and natural philosophy, in other words the science of their day. The afternoons were devoted to public debate or *disputio*, when the Master set a subject, a given Question, for debate, which the students then argued for and against, thesis and antithesis, with the Master determining the winner. The audience could also throw in questions, so the disputants were kept on their toes. This was also the nature of their writings, the supreme example of which is the *Summa Theologica* of Saint Thomas Aquinas. A question was posed, the objection was explored before the refutation was given. All this encouraged the active exploration of both the natural world as well as the world of faith and the students had to have a firm grasp not only of their faith but also the objections to it.

Death of Reginald

Such was the profound movement Dominic initiated in settling his houses wherever there was a university. He returned from his visitation of his foundations by way of Prouille, and arranged for his wise and trusty companion Bertrand of Carrigua to go to Toulouse as their prior to encourage and support the brothers in their trials. Following Reginald's success at Bologna, Dominic sent him to Paris, much to the sadness of the brothers at Bologna and the joy of those in Paris. When he preached, the streets of Paris were deserted. Matthew of France, who had been a student when Reginald had been a professor in Paris, and knew the acclaim and affluence he enjoyed then, asked him how he found the austerity, and deprivations of his new life now. Reginald assured him that he found his new life sweet and easy, and the greatest sweetness was to preach and to draw young men after him into such a fulfilling life. 'I do not consider myself worthy of anything in this Order,' he said, 'for I have been nothing but pleased with it.' That life, though, was drawing to a close, and as Dominic returned to Rome, he heard that Reginald had died, in the early part of March, 1220. On the night of his death, his disciple, Jordan, had a vision in which he saw a ship in the middle of the ocean, which then sank, but the Dominican brothers on board all reached the shore safely. He was later to understand that the ship was Reginald, but the brothers would survive the great loss they experienced at his death.

Dominic, too, was deeply grieved at the loss of such a luminary, but there were now new challenges awaiting him in Rome.

CHAPTER 8

NUNS AND LAITY

In Rome itself, Pope Honorius gave Dominic a new task that would probably be more of a miracle than converting the Saracens, that would need all the charism, charm and persuasion that he possessed. Honorius had wanted to establish a community of nuns at St Sixtus, drawing religious from different convents under the guidance of the Gilbertine Order, but, faced with women who did not want to be pressured into obeying religious discipline, prelates, priests and the Pope himself had found themselves powerless. He therefore gave St. Sixtus to the Dominican brothers for their house. Even so, Honorius was not one to yield too easily, and he handed the task to Dominic. There were several convents in Rome which were a law unto themselves, with women who had no vocation to the religious life. They could be the younger daughters without marriage prospects, widows who thought that retirement to a convent would enable them to live a genteel and undemanding life, and who liked to come and go as they pleased. They belonged to powerful Roman families who supported them vociferously in their opposition to a structured religious life. Those who opposed any change declared that they were following ancient customs that could not be changed, to which one of Dominic's early biographers remarked. 'The custom was indeed so very ancient that it could barely keep its legs. Moreover, we know well that there will always be ten thousand persons ready to do great things for relaxation and liberty but not one willing to stir a step for virtue.'

One of the most intransigent of the convents was the monastery of St. Mary-beyond-the-Tiber. Since Honorius had originally intended St. Sixtus to house nuns, Dominic suggested that the brothers should move out to Santa Sabina on the Aventine and give St. Sixtus to the nuns. The nuns, from the Abbess down, declared they would not move for anyone, not even for the Pope and all his Cardinals. Furthermore, they added piously, they had a miraculous picture of Our Lady, said to have been painted by St. Luke the Evangelist himself. The picture liked being where it was, since it had arrived miraculously in the first place, and was greatly venerated by the Romans. On his second visit, Dominic managed to persuade the Abbess about the advantages of the move, and she managed to win over the nuns, under one condition, that the picture came with them. If the picture transferred itself back to St. Mary's then so would the nuns—it had already decided to stay at the Lateran with Pope Sergius 111 and had transferred itself of its own accord back to St. Mary's.

To firm up their resolution, Dominic required them to make profession at his hands, and forbade them to leave the monastery. He left them, hoping that they were more settled, but it was not to be. Tongues started wagging, criticising this upstart, this scoundrel and ignorant friar, and the nuns changed their minds. He left them for a few days and then went to say Mass for them; afterwards, assembling them together, he spoke plainly: 'I am well aware, my daughters,' he said, 'that you have repented of the promise you gave me, and now desire to withdraw from the ways of God. Therefore, let those of you who are truly and spontaneously willing to go to St. Sixtus make their Profession over again in my hands.'

The nuns had just come from attending Dominic's Mass. He was unable to say Mass without tears of devotion running down his cheeks, absorbed in the great mystery of which he was a minister. It must have been a moving experience that would have shaken them from their complacency. Now they were faced with his eloquence, his charm and his utter devotion in following Christ. The Abbess at once renewed her vows and the rest of the community followed, making their profession as Dominican nuns. Dominic had succeeded where a Pope had failed.

However, he was also shrewd, and took the precaution of taking possession of the keys to the monastery and appointing some of his lay brothers as porters. On Ash Wednesday the Cardinals assembled to witness the Abbess hand over the office and authority to Dominic.

The occasion of the profession ceremony also witnessed a miracle. Dominic was called outside where the nephew of one of the bishops had been thrown from his horse and lay dead in the square. The bishop fainted on hearing the news, as the boy's badly mangled body was carried inside. Dominic celebrated Mass, but afterwards he came into the room where the body had been laid out, ordered everyone to leave the room, prayed over the body and restored the boy to life.

Four days later, on the first Sunday of Lent, the nuns took possession of their new convent, a ceremony that was attended by lay people as well as religious. One young woman of seventeen, Cecilia Cesarini, of a noble Roman family, came to Dominic and threw herself at his feet, begging to be clothed in the habit. Other young women followed her example. She was the Sister Cecilia who gave us the portrait of Saint Dominic and other incidences of his life.

That night, under the cover of darkness so as not to rouse the interest and possible opposition of the Roman populace, a small barefoot procession of Dominic, two Cardinals and others, carried the portrait of Our Lady from St Mary's to St. Sixtus. The portrait stayed where it was in its new home, and so did the nuns.

On the second Sunday of Lent Dominic was preaching in the nun's church when he was interrupted by a possessed woman in the crowd crying out, 'Villain! These nuns were once mine, and you have robbed me of all but one, and that one is mine! We are seven in number and we have her in our keeping.'

Dominic ordered the woman to be silent, making the sign of the cross over her, delivering her from the demonic possession, witnessed by the large crowd. A few days later the woman sought him out and begged to be received into the convent. He gave her the name of Amata (loved) as a perpetual reminder of God's love for her.

Establishing the Nuns

With the nuns established at St. Sixtus and the brothers at the basilica of Santa Sabina, which would be, from then on, the mother-house of the Order, Dominic had a heavy workload, introducing the brothers and the sisters to the discipline and ethos of religious life. He sent for eight nuns from Prouille to join the St. Sixtus community, to introduce them to genuine religious observance, and Dominic himself gave them regular instruction. Dominic was just as concerned for the formation of the nuns as he was for his brothers, because he was adamant that they were just as much Preachers as the men—not in the pulpit, but by their lives of dedication and love for God. From the very beginning they should have just as much training in theology and spirituality so that their spiritual life should have access to all the rich treasury of the Church down the ages to inform their life of prayer and service.

'In the evenings Dominic came to the nuns,' Sister Cecilia testified. 'He would give them a conference or a homily in the presence of the brethren, and he taught them about the Order, for they had no other teacher to form them to the life of the Order.'

Sister Cecilia recounts one of those visits, when Dominic arrived late for his conference and the nuns had retired to bed. When the brother rang the bell that was the signal that Dominic had come, they hastened to the church where Dominic was waiting for them. He explained that he was late because he had been fishing—for souls—and had landed a good catch, one Gaudius, who entered the Order and later went to Siena. When he had finished his homily, he asked the sisters if they could give him something to drink. The cellarer went and brought him a cup and wine, and when the brother had filled it to the brim, Dominic drank all of it, then handed the cup to the brothers, and then to the nuns, and all the time the cup remained full to the brim, even when they handed the cup back to him.

The sisters were concerned that as it was late at night by then, it would be dangerous for the brothers to return to Santa Sabina, for fear of cut-throats and thieves, but Dominic reassured them, adamant that they had to return. 'The Lord absolutely wants me to go,' he said, 'and he will send his angel with us.' He was right. At the door of the church stood a beautiful young man who went before them, with Dominic behind the rest of the brothers— another guardian angel! The locked door of the church opened before him, and closed tight again when they had all entered, and then the angel left them. When the bell for Matins rang, the other brothers were amazed to find them already there, with the church doors locked.

Touchingly, when he made a visitation to Spain he brought back as a present spoons made of cypress for each of the nuns.

Unity of the Dominican Family

The situation that arose shortly after Dominic's death underlined the importance of the nuns to the Dominican family. In Germany, many more young women joined the Order than the friars could cope with, to give them the necessary oversight. Some, unsuited to the religious life, were being admitted without due scrutiny, and there was subsequent chaos in the convents. The friars felt they were being taken away from their proper work of preaching and teaching to be chaplains and advisers to the convents, and felt that the women's convents should be placed under the jurisdiction of the bishops. Blessed Jordan had been elected Master of the Order after Dominic's death and he absolutely opposed the suggestion because it would have destroyed the unity of the Order. However, he sought the advice of the universities and put the proposal to the 1224

General Chapter that met in Paris and the verdict was unanimous—the Pope himself had given the jurisdiction of the nuns to the Order, and this arrangement should not be overturned.

This settled the matter until four years later, when the 1228 Chapter laid down that the friars should not be burdened with direction of nunneries, without making it clear that this applied to the houses of other Orders, not to the Dominican nuns. Although the matter was brought up again over the years, the matter was settled definitively in 1267 by the Pope, and the nuns remained permanently under the jurisdiction of the friars.

This might seem a matter of law and regulations, but there was a fundamental principle at stake. The nuns are a vital and irreplaceable part of the Dominican family. They are the prayer lungs, as it were, of the Order, ensuring that there is the deep, hidden spring of union with God in intercessory prayer that undergirds the brothers' preaching and active ministry. Each person is called to a prayerful life in conjunction with the active life that should flow from in it, in whatever way the Lord willed for that particular person, but the Church has always recognised the importance the contemplative life has within the whole life of the Church.

Diana d'Andaló

While Dominic was in Bologna for the General Chapter in 1218, he was eager to found a house of nuns there. He spent the night in prayer and the following day consulted the brothers about the matter, who confirmed him in this purpose. They found a suitable site for the house, but the bishop of Bologna refused permission for it to be built as it was too close to the city. At the same time he met Diana d'Andaló, whose father had donated St. Nicholas of the Vineyards to the friars, with the one stipulation that Diana should not become a nun. Worldly, of outstanding beauty, high spirited, charming and feisty, full of the joy of life, she would not have contemplated such a step until the arrival of Master Reginald to Bologna. She came to listen to his sermons more out of curiosity than for edification, but when he gave a sermon, quoting from Saint Peter and Saint Paul on worldliness and extravagance of dress, she received a profound change of heart. She went to Confession with Reginald and immediately, with the spontaneity characteristic of her, changed her life completely. Beneath her sumptuous clothes and jewels she wore a hair shirt and an iron chain round her waist, and led a prayerful life within the parameters of her secular life. She sought Dominic's counsel, and with some of her companions made a vow of virginity to him. He was delighted when she confided her desire to be a nun and undoubtedly saw her as a future inmate in his monastery.

In 1219 she made a vow of self-consecration before Reginald, and although she continued to live her religious life in the world Diana yearned for the religious life and was in no wise to be deterred from her ideal. She waited patiently for the right time to act. On 22 July 1221, Feast Day of Saint Mary Magdalene, she said she wanted to visit the convent of Ronzano, a hermitage belonging to the Canonesses of St. Mark of Mantua. She arrived with great pomp with a retinue of her lady attendants, but once there she went to the sisters' dormitory and asked to be clothed in the habit. Her request was granted, but when her ladies realised what had happened they sent word to her family back in Bologna. Immediately her furious father, with a crowd of friends and relatives, besieged the convent and dragged her out with such force that they broke some of her ribs. Her injuries kept her bedridden for a year, but her resolve was unbroken.

Dominic was deeply saddened to hear of her illness and while she was bedridden wrote letters to her secretly, since her father would not allow her to speak to anyone without a member of the family being present. Sadly, he died before the plan could be realised, but when Diana recovered from her injuries she once again slipped out of her father's house on the Feast of All Saints and made her way once again to Ronzano. This time, her family did not pursue her as they realised that it was useless to thwart such a determined character.

Foundation of Nuns at Bologna

It was not until after Dominic's death that his successor, Jordan of Saxony, was to fulfil Dominic's dream of founding a house for the nuns in Bologna. By this time Diana's family were willing to support the brothers and gave them a site in Valparaiso, where they built the convent, later called Mount Saint Agnes. During the Octave of the Ascension 1223, the brothers solemnly escorted Diana from her hermitage to her new home, with four other noble ladies from Bologna. On the Feast of Saints Peter and Paul they were clothed in the Dominican habit.

It was not long before nobles ladies flocked to the monastery. At first, it was a form of 'double monastery', in which priests and lay brothers had their quarters in the convent complex, in order to say Mass for the nuns, give them spiritual direction, attend to their temporal affairs and the external work of the convent. This arrangement gradually evolved with just a priest saying Mass for them and attending to their spiritual needs without being bound to the convent itself.

For the thirteen years until her death that she was their founding Prioress, Diana led a fervent and dedicated community. The chronicles of the monastery give a beautiful and touching testimony to her:

> This happy woman was extremely sensible and well spoken, with a beautiful face and an attractive appearance, charming and lovable. She was upright, devoted to the worship of God, intent on prayer, and so given to devotion that she often moved her sisters to tears to observe her. She was a great lover of the brethren and of the Order. She was deeply humble in her own mind, and wore a cheaper habit than anyone else; she was remarkably enthusiastic for religious observance in herself and others. She was a wonderful asset to the monastery she had founded, both by her words and by her example.

Diana and Jordan

Between Jordan of Saxony and such an outstanding woman there developed a deep love and affection. His travels as Master meant that they were rarely able to meet face to face, so instead their relationship was lived out through correspondence that is one of the literary pearls of the Middle Ages.[12] The letters he wrote to her were intended not only for her own spiritual development, but contained much good advice for Diana's governance of her community and for the nuns under her care. He was impressed by their fervour and their austerity, but recognised that everything had to be done prudently. They should fight the spiritual battle with prudence when they sought to subdue their human nature to their divine calling, but this does not happen overnight,

> but little by little, advancing by measured steps in the way of the virtues, not trying to fly but by climbing cautiously up the scale of perfection, till at length you come to the summit of all perfection . . . in all things you should observe moderation, only the love of God knows neither measure nor moderation. And that love is nourishing not by the afflicting of the flesh but by holy desires and loving contemplation and through the cherishing of that sisterly love by which each of you loves the others as herself.[13]

Third Order for Lay People

One of the interesting developments was the number of secular ladies and assistants who attached themselves to the convent, without them entering as religious. This seems to be the development of the Dominican Third Order, in which lay men and women became members of the Order

---

[12] Vid. To Heaven with Diana ed. Gerald Vann O.P.

[13] Letter 10, January 1225, To Heaven with Diana

while living their life in the world. Saint Francis of Assisi had already paved the way for this with his introduction of the Franciscan Third Order; a necessity, since so many people were flocking to his Order, that some feared the whole of Italy would become friars or nuns! By introducing a Third Order, lay men and women could remain 'in the world', following their usual professions and work, yet sharing in the Dominican charism.

The establishment of Third Orders met a need that had previously been met by the heretical sects, the Waldensians and the Cathars, for example. The simplicity of life and the embrace of poverty for the love of God, where the poverty of their daily lives could be given meaning, were now evident in the Church. People did not have to go to the sects to see the Gospel lived out in the lives of their preachers and teachers. Bishops, priests, religious, were setting the example. It is sad that the Crusades had to bring in suppression by force, for the influence of the sects was being weakened anyway by this revolution. Further, the Dominicans were giving the people the strong theological foundation they needed to sustain their faith and to see through the errors of the heretics. Based firmly on the Scriptures, their teaching could nourish the people in their spiritual life and bring them to the holiness and union with God that is the goal of every Christian life; a holiness that is manifest in so many of them, as the roll call of the Saints and Blesseds of the Dominican, Franciscan and Carmelite Orders, for example, attest.

With the Dominican Third Order, we have already seen how Conrad, bishop of Porto, said that he considered himself a Dominican at heart although belonging to another Order. There was also Cardinal William of Sabina, who was a Carthusian, but who wished to be attached also to the Dominicans; he greatly helped them in the affairs of the Order.

This extended the scope of the Order, among women especially, since they could engage in social activities such as teaching, nursing, social work of all kinds, when religious life for women for several centuries meant entering an enclosed Order. Some one hundred and fifty years later, with the Third Order well established, Saint Catherine of Siena joined their ranks, becoming the first woman Doctor of the Church. She was instrumental in bringing back the Pope to Rome from his exile in Avignon.

The Third Order was also called the Militia of Christ, and some of the laymen did indeed take up arms in the Crusades against the Saracens, with Dominic's approval. Although Dominic wanted only peaceful means used against heretics, it was a different situation when it came to the defence of the Holy Land and the holy places, and in defence of Christians who were enduring persecution under Muslim domination.

CHAPTER 9

THE FIRST BOLOGNA CHAPTER

On 17 May 1220, the Feast of Pentecost, Dominic convened the first Chapter of the Order at Bologna. Delegates came from France, Italy, Spain and Poland; since the Order had been existence for only four years, this shows how rapidly it had spread.

Among those who attended was Blessed Jordan, who had recently been professed, and he gave details of the Chapter proceedings. The first concern of the delegates was to approve the Rule. Dominic had noted, on his travels, that sometimes the Rule was being observed almost too scrupulously. There is an anecdote that one night at Bologna itself, a brother was seized by an invisible, diabolic hand and cried out for help. All thirty brothers ran to his aid but were in their turn dragged and thrown around the choir. Reginald then arrived and delivered the brother. All this happened without a word spoken, so scrupulously did they observe the Great Silence, that period of the night in religious orders when silence was observed with even greater care.

Dominic stressed, though, that the Rule should not bind under sin but only under penalty, for 'if any were to believe the contrary, he would waste no time in going through the cloisters and cut to pieces with a knife all the rules'. The Rule had to be at the service of their primary aim, the preaching of the Gospel, and not an end in itself.

Democracy

His next concern was to establish democratic government, where every brother was to have an equal voice. As Humbert of Romans expressed it, 'What touches all must be approved by all.' The office of Master General should not be held for life, as in the monastic orders of the time, but should be elected for a set period. Dominic held the office himself at the time, and decided that they should vote then and there for a new Master—his humility prompted him to this, since he felt himself unworthy of the office, but he had also never relinquished his dream of going to Tartary; to be free of the office might bring that dream nearer. The brothers duly exercised their democratic right and voted for Dominic.

Property

Until now the brothers had been given property and churches in which to make their foundations, but they now resolved to accept alms. This resolution had to be modified in time, but poverty remained a basic characteristic of the Order. Not all the brothers were happy with the extreme poverty practiced by Dominic himself, though. Some of them arrived on horses, and tradition says that Dominic promptly sold the horses.

Just after the General Chapter had ended Dominic discovered to his horror that a grand convent was being built there and called the procurator, Rudolph of Faenza to him, saying, 'Will you build palaces while I'm still alive?' he asked. 'If you do, you will bring ruin on the Order.' Nobody dared to continue building it until after his death.

Poverty

Poverty was a moot point. Many religious houses had become very wealthy, although the reasons for this should be seen in their historical perspective. Europe was just emerging from what is called the 'Dark Ages'—although recent research has shown that they were not as dark as all that—and the chaos that ensued with the collapse of the Roman Empire. Monasteries and the Church became the most stable elements in this period of transition, men and women flocked to them, and the discipline of manual work carried out collectively in the religious life provided the best blueprint for agriculture and crafts. On the other hand, they were also the charitable institutes of their day, providing food, clothing, educational and other resources for the poorest people.

How to follow the happy mean then, of poverty, between the extreme poverty of a Saint Francis, that only a few of his followers could emulate, and the wealth of the great abbeys? (Some of the brothers must have been made uneasy by the sight of Saint Francis, when he visited Bologna, so angered by the grand convent that his brothers had built to emulate that of the Dominicans, that he began to strip the roof off with his bare hands.

He desisted only when it was pointed out to him that the convent did not belong to him but to the town.)

The cells of the brothers were regulated to reflect the poverty and simplicity of the Order. It was stipulated that in each one there should be a crucifix and an image of Our Lady. Dominic's deep love of the Mother of God became a hallmark of the Order and devotion to her is central to Dominican spirituality. Four centuries later, at another General Chapter at Bologna, it was decreed that the Litany of Loretto should be recited after the *Salve Regina* in the Saturday Office in all the convents, and also that the invocation 'Queen of the Most Holy Rosary should be added to it.

Lay Brothers

In their lengthy discussions, the principle was laid down that poverty should, once again, be at the service of their main purpose and charism, that of preaching, and of the Gospel and the witness that it would give. Dominic proposed that the priests should be excused from all work that interfered with their preaching and their study, and the necessary manual work connected with the upkeep of the houses be left to the lay brothers. The Chapter agreed that agriculture, crafts and other work that was an essential part of Orders such as the Benedictines was not part of Dominican life, but they voted down Dominic's proposal that the ordinary work of the house be left to lay brothers. All should take their turn and thus keep their feet on the ground as a necessary balance to their life of study, preaching and prayer.

This did not mean that he considered the lay brothers inferior in their religious life. They were equally entitled to the name of Preacher, because they preached eloquently by their life of dedication and simplicity. They were invaluable in helping with building the convents that were springing up everywhere, and they accompanied the priests on their preaching tours. This meant that the priests were able to spread out more widely, supported as they were by the lay brothers. With the nuns, they witnessed to what was called the 'silent preaching' of their lives.

Further Missions

From the very beginning, Dominic had been keen for the friars to spread out as far as possible in their mission of preaching, and requests had been received from England, Scotland and Ireland, as well as Morocco and other countries in the Near East. Because the need and the danger of the latter were greater, brothers were to be sent there first. However, there were dangers nearer home, for the brothers preaching in the Languedoc and in the newly established mission in the north of Italy, were coming under murderous attack. When the call came, Dominic himself went to Italy to support them in their ministry.

The Nuns

He did not forget his nuns, and during the Chapter wrote to the nuns at the newly founded monastery at Madrid, giving them practical instructions as to the good order of the convent, but also encouraging them in the austerity of their lives:

'I am delighted at the fervour with which you follow your holy way of life,' he wrote to them, 'and thank God for it. Fight the good fight, my daughters, against your ancient foe, fight him insistently with fasting, because no one will win the crown of victory without engaging in the contest in the proper way.'

Dominic was urging them to fight, not only for victory over evil in their own lives, but because they were supporting the brothers who were preparing to go, or who had already gone into danger to preach the Gospel. The nuns were fulfilling their particular vocation as preachers in supporting them by their prayer and fasting and austerity.

CHAPTER 10

PRAYER AND VOCATIONS

Understandably, given the publicity of the General Chapter, men flocked to the Order. John of Vicenza was studying law at the University, but gave it up to enter the Dominicans when he heard Dominic preach. Thomas of Pagilo's family were so opposed to his vocation that they stripped the habit off him and forced him to wear his former worldly garments. Dominic went into the church to pray for him, and Thomas began to cry out that the clothes were burning him. 'Take these from me,' he cried, 'and give me back my habit!' His frightened relatives ran off and the young man hastened back to the convent where he put on his coarse woollen habit, at which the burning sensation ceased.

On the Feast of the Assumption Dominic was talking to a close friend, a Cistercian prior, and said that he had never prayed for anything that he had not received. 'Then I'm surprised that you haven't prayed for the vocation of Master Conrad the German, because the brothers have long wanted him to join them.' That night the two of them kept vigil in the church, and before the hour of Prime Conrad came into the church and asked for the habit.

Peter of Aubenas

Peter of Aubenas was practicing medicine in Genoa when he made a promise to join the Waldensians, as the Poor Men of Lyons were often called. He was attracted by the outward signs of their humility and virtue, while he considered the friars as too cheerful and showy. However, he was torn in his mind and one evening knelt in prayer to ask the Lord what he should do. He then went to sleep and had a dream in which he saw himself walking down a road with a dark wood on the left hand side, in which he saw Waldensians with sad, solemn faces all going their different ways. This is an interesting prophecy at this point in the dream, for at that time the Waldensians had received approval from the Pope, with the proviso that they should engage in preaching only with the approval of the local bishop. When they disobeyed this injunction they rapidly parted from the Church, so that they did indeed go separate ways.

Then, in his dream, Peter saw on the right hand side a beautiful high wall. He walked along it until he came to a gate, and through it saw a beautiful, flower-strewn meadow in which he saw a crowd of Friars Preachers gathered in a ring, with joyful faces raised to heaven. One of them was holding the Sacred Host aloft. The sight so delighted him that he wanted to enter the gate and join them, but was prevented from doing so by an angel blocking his way. 'You will not enter in here now,' the angel told him. The dream ended with Peter bathed in tears, but a few days later, after he had wound up his affairs, he joyfully entered the Friars Preachers.

There were also the young men Reginald attracted into the Order. Among them was Brother Robaldo, who preached in Milan with great success against the heretics; Bonviso of Piacenza testified at Dominic's canonisation; Stephen of Spain was one of those received into the Order by Dominic. He went to confession to the saint and, as he said, 'I thought that he loved me.' Later that evening, while he was at supper with friends Dominic sent two friars to him with an urgent summons. Stephen knelt at his feet and received the habit then and there and said often, 'I have never thought of this without astonishment.'

Jordan of Saxony

Another young man was to enter and bring even greater glory to the Order—Blessed Jordan of Saxony, whom we have already met, who came into the Order through the influence of Master Reginald. When in March 1220 Reginald died, he left behind a worthy successor.

Jordan of Saxony was one of the most famous and brilliant of the young men who entered the Order and was the Order's first biographer. Born of a noble family from Westphalia, he studied at the University of Paris, and then lectured as a Master. He had thought long about a vocation, speaking of it with Dominic when the saint had been in Paris. Reginald also was a great inspiration to him, but he waited until he could persuade his great friend, Henry of Utrecht, to enter with him. They were both clothed with the habit towards the end of Lent, and Jordan received a vision that pointed to the place he would have in the Order. He saw a clear and sparkling fountain that sprang up suddenly in the church of Saint James and just as suddenly it ceased. Then a clear stream appeared in place of the fountain, the waters of which flowed in immense waves until they filled the whole world. By this, Jordan understood that the dying fountain was Reginald. As for Jordan, it is said that in his lifetime he clothed more than a thousand novices in the habit. He was elected unanimously as Master of the Order after Dominic's death, and showed himself a wise, humane and cultured man, and a much-sought after spiritual director.

Dominic in Community

Time and again, when mentioning the young men who flocked to the Dominicans, Dominic's prayer is at the heart of it. Whatever decision he made, whenever he was approached by one seeking admission to the Order, he resorted to prayer to discern the will of the Lord on each particular occasion. He had an individual love, care and concern for each one of them. Dominic attracted men to him by the charm and the holiness of his life, but at the heart was his life of prayer and union with God.

He was deeply loved in every community in which he stayed. If he had cause to correct a brother he would not do so immediately but would wait and take the brother aside privately and corrected him with so much love and gentleness that the brother was not humiliated but eager to improve with greater zeal, and accepted the penance for the fault Dominic would impose.

Novices, especially, appreciated the care and encouragement he gave to them, as they embarked on their difficult and austere life. 'When I was a novice', Brother Stephen of Spain testified, 'I suffered a great many trials, but I endured them all at the encouragement of the holy man. The same thing happened to many of the novices, as they told me.'

Joy

Dominican life was austere, but as so often, such austerity, when embraced for the love of God and of souls, was surrounded by joy. The account of Peter Aubenas' conversion shows that cheerfulness and joy were seen as characteristic of the friars by those who knew them. Dominic himself was a supreme example of this and made it a trademark of his Order. The story is told of some novices, in Jordan of Saxony's time, who were overcome by the giggles during Compline and were rebuked by one of the senior brothers. However, 'Laugh to your heart's content,' responded Jordan, 'and don't stop because of that brother's rebuke. You have my full leave, and it is only right that you should laugh after breaking free from the devil's bondage. So laugh on, and be as merry as you please.'

Poverty

Dominic wanted his Order to be poor, and he himself set the greatest example of poverty. His habit was made out of coarse, though clean material, and an embarrassingly short scapular. His habit was a mass of patches and darns, and he never owned more than one, which he wore day and night, the same habit in summer and winter.

Prayer in the Night

Perhaps we have to go to those nights Dominic spent in prayer before his Lord in the Blessed Sacrament to seek an answer to the rapid growth of his Order and its efficacy in winning souls. His groans and prayers were so loud that they would wake up the brothers, they were the groans of the Holy Spirit within him, too deep for words. Those who knew him witnessed to the depth of his compassion; as he approached a town who would pray over it, pray for the inhabitants, the tears flowing with love and yearning for their eternal salvation, the motive that drove him on to seek out the lost sheep to bring them back to the Lord. Then in the watches of the night, he would bring them before his Lord, and the men and women who were flocking into the Order to follow as preachers in his footsteps.

Dominic the Hidden Light

Dominic was a preacher, whose words were meant for those who listened to him, and we possess only three short letters of his. No-one wrote down his sermons and we have only some reminiscences of those who knew him, mostly the testimonies given during the canonisation proceedings. Since these followed a set format they are somewhat repetitive. He was indeed a hidden light, like the lamp glowing quietly before the tabernacle, before the presence of the Lord. He always hidden—the faithful lieutenant of Bishop Diego, labouring almost alone in the Languedoc, ensuring that others would lead his Order, spreading out into areas that he would never see. He had only six years to live when he founded his Order, and to a great extent depended on the outstanding characters that joined it. Therefore, his real life was the one led in the darkness of the night, where he prayed unceasingly, and it is this prayer that ensured the amazing fecundity of his Order and its influence ever since.

Brother Paul of Venice testified that he never remembered Dominic speaking either in detraction or of flattery of anyone, no idle or malicious word. He was either in prayer or speaking of God. He never saw him angry, upset or troubled, even when tired out by his travels. 'He never gave way to passion,' Brother Paul said, 'but was always calm, joyful in tribulations and patient in adversity.'

This is what Blessed Jordan of Saxony wrote of him, summing up his character and the impression he made on others:

> His exceptional character and burning zeal revealed him as a chosen, precious vessel. His equanimity and calmness was disturbed only when moved to compassion and mercy. Because a joyful heart shows itself in a cheerful face, he showed the peace and tranquillity of his heart. He was firm and resolute in the decisions he made, and rarely changed his mind. There was something so very special about the radiance and joy that shone from his face that he captivated everyone as soon as they saw him.
>
> Whether he was with prince or prelate, with strangers he met on his way, or with his brothers, his talk was only of that which

would draw his hearers towards love of Christ and away from worldly things. Always his words and actions were that of a man of the Gospel. During the day there was no-one more friendly and approachable to his brothers and those he met.

Description of Dominic

Sister Cecilia, who received the Dominican habit from him, has left a description of him that would not have changed much during his fairly short life:

> He was of medium height, of slight build, with a beautiful face, slightly ruddy complexion, and slightly red hair and beard; his eyes were beautiful. There was a kind of radiance about his forehead and between his eyebrows, which attracted everyone to respect and love him. He was always cheerful and happy, except when he was moved to compassion by any kind of suffering on the part of his neighbour. He had long beautiful hands, and a powerful, beautiful, resonant voice. He never went bald, but had a complete ring of hair round his tonsure, with just a sprinkling of grey.

Above all, despite his profound and self-effacing humility, or perhaps because of it, there was something special about him that endeared and charmed those who met him and encouraged countless numbers to follow him into an austere yet joyful life, from all parts of society, professors, students, peasants, men, women, united in the love of God.

CHAPTER 11

DEATH OF DOMINIC

At the beginning of May, as the brothers were travelling towards Bologna for the next General Chapter, Pope Honorius sent a letter to the heads of six of the Religious Orders informing them that he had placed into the hands of Dominic the task of preaching to the heretics, and wished that they join him in this enterprise. As soon as the Chapter had finished, Dominic set off for Lombardy where the Albigensians were deeply entrenched, and then journeyed on to Venice.

In May the following year he returned to Bologna for the second General Chapter. This time Jordan was not present, as the Chapter had appointed him as Provincial of Lombardy. By this time the Order had grown so rapidly that it was necessary to give it more structure, and it was divided into five Provinces. The primary result was to send friars out even further afield, to Hungary, Germany, Poland, Norway, Sweden, and also to England. Paul of Hungary was chosen to lead the mission to Hungary, and the band of brothers were so eager to set out that they left before the Chapter had ended, somehow knowing that the mission would end in martyrdom. Friars also set out for England to found a house in Oxford, the country's intellectual capital at that time, so that the Dominicans would have foundations in all the great universities of the West. The band of thirteen friars arrived in Oxford on 15 August 1221, Feast of the Assumption, and they soon found ready recruits among the students and masters already at the University.

Dominic stayed in Bologna a further few days after the Chapter ended to receive the citizenship of the city, and then, on June 7th, he once more set out on his preaching mission, to northern Italy, with Venice as his first destination. While there, he met his old friend, Cardinal Conti, who perhaps remarked on the contrast between his venerable age and the still quite young Dominic. But Dominic was tired, and even before the Chapter had received a premonition that his earthly journey was drawing to its end. 'You see me now in health,' he replied to Cardinal Conti, 'but before the next Feast of the Assumption I shall be with God.' In Bergamo he suffered the first of several attacks of fever, and when he arrived back in Bologna at the end of July the brothers were shocked by how much he had aged. His hair had thinned and there were sprinkles of grey in his tonsure. Even so, he talked late into the night with the Prior and with Brother Rudolph, the procurator about the affairs of the Order. Seeing his fatigue they tried to persuade him not to come to matins, but to rest, but he would not hear of it. He kept vigil beforehand, and then joined the community for the Divine Office, the last time he was able to do so. After Matins he admitted that he had a headache, but still would not rest in bed, only on a straw mattress

The unhealthy air of Bologna was not doing him good, and he suffered from heat exhaustion, so they moved him to a Benedictine priory, Saint Mary of the Mountain, higher up and away from the oppressive heat of the city, where he received extreme unction The rector saw some benefit from having a saint dying in their midst and being buried in their churchyard, saying as much within Dominic's hearing. Dominic replied he would not stay there as he wanted, he said, to die 'beneath the feet of my brethren. Take me home to the vineyard, and no-one will be able to oppose my being buried among my own.' The brothers fashioned a makeshift stretcher and carried his emaciated body, racked with fever and dysentery, carefully back to St. Nicholas, back to his own community. He still had no cell of his own, so they put him in the cell of Brother Moneta. When he realised that they had laid him on some form of bed he insisted that they lay him on the ground, on sacking.

It was August 6th and he realised he was dying; he asked for twelve of his brethren to come to him so that he could say a few last words to them. He exhorted them to be zealous in promoting the Order, to persevere in holiness and told them to be very circumspect in their association with women, in order to avoid even the hint of scandal. Then, touchingly, he confessed that although the grace of God had kept him in purity of life, 'yet I confess that I did not escape the fault that talks with young women affected my heart more than conversations with those who were older.' He then left them his legacy, a spiritual legacy, for that was all he possessed:

My very dear brothers,' he said, 'this is what I leave you as a possession to be held by right of inheritance to you, my children. Have charity, preserve humility and possess voluntary poverty.' He could not leave them a possession that he did not have himself.

To lessen their grief he assured them that he would be of more benefit to them after death than in life, for he had entrusted his labours and his fruitful life to One who knew well how to keep it to eternal life. In heaven his power to obtain answers to his prayer would be even more powerful because he would be even more firmly rooted in the Lord's power.

He made a general confession and received the last rites. The Prior, Father Ventura, recommended them all to his prayers, and then, in a gesture he had used so often in the past, he raised up his arms to heaven and began his final prayers on earth, which so closely mirrored his Lord's prayer at the Last Supper. The words of Scripture, which had permeated his whole life, did not desert him now: 'Holy Father, you know that with all my heart I have remained steadfast in your will, and those whom you have given me I have guarded and kept. I commend them to you. Do you keep and guard them.' He then whispered, 'Begin' as he entered into his death agony. As the assembled community began the prayers for the dying Friar Rudolph wiped away the sweat on his face as his brothers wept.

As they came to the words, 'Come to his assistance, you saints of God. Come forth to meet him, angels of the Lord. Receive his soul and present it to God Most High,' Dominic breathed his last and entered into the longed-for presence of his Lord.

CHAPTER 12

LIFE AFTER DEATH

The brothers laid his body in a wooden coffin and buried him under the entrance of the choir in the church of Saint Nicholas. His great friend, Cardinal Ugolino, was in Bologna at the time and celebrated the Requiem Mass, assisted by the Patriarch of Aquileia and other prelates.

Albert, prior of Saint Catherine of Bologna, was a great and close friend of Dominic, and was overcome by grief during the funeral. He then saw that there was an air of calm joyousness among the friars, and he reflected that, his own grief of loss notwithstanding, sadness was out of place when a saint has been united in glory with the Lord he so loved and served on earth. He then went up to the bier and kissed the body of his friend, and found himself filled with a serene joy. He went up to the prior of Saint Nicholas and clasped his hands. 'Dear Father, rejoice with me,' he said. 'Master Dominic has just spoken to me and assured me that before the end of the year we will all be re-united in Christ.' Dominic spoke truly, for both died before the end of the year.

That Dominic was in heaven few would deny. Father Guallo Romanoni, prior of the convent in Brescia, received a vision that assured him of that. Leaning against the bell tower of the church he fell asleep and dreamt that he saw two ladders being let down from above. At the top of one stood Our Lord, at the top of the other was Our Lady, with angels ascending and descending the ladders. At the foot of the ladder was a friar, his face covered with his hood, as it is in death. When the ladders were drawn back up to heaven he saw the face of the friar, his face radiant with glory, surrounded by angels, who placed him at the feet of Jesus. He understood that it was Dominic, now in glory.

Others also received visions and confirmations that Dominic was with his Lord. Brother Raoul, as he was celebrating Mass, saw in vision a long road leading out of Bologna. Dominic was walking along it, crowned with a golden coronet and dazzling with light, accompanied by two venerable men.

On the night following the funeral, a University student who had been deeply devoted to Dominic, but was unable to attend the funeral also had a vision of him sitting in the church of St. Nicholas, radiant with glory. The vision was so vivid that he exclaimed, 'What, are you still here, Master Dominic?'

'Yes,' came the reply. 'I live, indeed, because God has granted me eternal life in heaven.'

The Cause for his Canonisation

Dominic had long been revered as a saint even before his death, and now crowds flocked to his tomb; miracles that had been frequent during his life now flowed in abundance. However, nothing was done to advance the cause for his canonisation. When one of the friars was questioned about this, he replied, 'What need is there for canonisation? God knows the holiness of Master Dominic; it matters little if it be declared publicly by man.'

It was not until twelve years later that the Bishop and the *Podestá*, or Mayor, of Bologna sent a delegation to the Pope to ask him to set up a board of enquiry into the holiness of Master Dominic, as he was known. This became a matter of urgency because the community had increased so much that the convent was in urgent need, not only of repairs but also to be enlarged. This meant that Dominic's tomb had to be opened up and the remains transferred into the church and placed in a marble tomb. The Pope's permission had to be obtained for this, and the Pope was now Dominic's old friend Cardinal Ugolino, who had been elected Pope in 1227 and taken the name of Gregory 1X. He, of course, was only too delighted to agree, and reproved the friars for being so tardy in bringing forward Dominic's cause for canonisation.

Translation of the Relics

The solemn translation took place 24 May 1233, during the Whitsuntide Chapter of the Order, under the Mastership of Blessed Jordan of Saxony. Three hundred friars had already gathered in Bologna. The Pope had hoped to be there himself, but was unable to do so, and appointed the Archbishop of Ravenna as his representative.

Many of the friars were concerned about the state the relics might be in, or even if they might be stolen, but Brother Nicholas of Giovanezzo received a consoling vision in which Dominic appeared to him, of majestic appearance, and said joyously to him, '*Hic accipiet benedictionem a Domino, et misericordiam a Deo salutari suo*'; 'This will receive God's blessing and mercy from the God of your salvation.'

To prevent the body from being stolen the tomb had been covered over with limestone and very hard cement, and a very thick, strong stone had been placed over the wooden coffin. The whole had to be broken up with pickaxes. The Father Provincial, who was overseeing the translation, ordained that no lay people should be present because he feared the smell that would emanate from the corpse, since water had already seeped into the coffin, but the *podesta,* with twenty four nobles, insisted on being present. To everyone's amazement, when the tomb was uncovered a most beautiful, pleasant scent came from the bones. The fragrance lasted for several days afterwards in the church, remaining on the bones and on the hands of those who had touched the relics, and even some three hundred years later witnesses affirmed that the scent still lingered.

On 13 July 1233 Pope Gregory sent a letter instituting a Commission of Enquiry, and two were set up, in Bologna and Toulouse. The first witnesses began to give their testimonies in August 1233, twelve years after Dominic's death.

Over three hundred men and women, religious, priests, nuns and lay people, testified at the two commissions, and at the end of the testimonies submitted by the Toulouse Commission, the three commissioners, Peter, Abbot of St. Saturninus, Raymond Donat, Archdeacon of St. Stephen's and Pons, archdeacon of St. Saturninus, ended: 'his holiness and virtues were universally recognized and publicly spoken of wherever he had visited during his lifetime'. Pope Gregory 1X canonised him in 1234.

EPILOGUE

Writing this book was a real voyage of discovery for me, to discover the real Dominic; I found it a daunting task. Was there any saint so elusive? Unlike Saint Teresa of Avila, whose writings we have and who wrote voluminous letters that so vividly reveal her character, Dominic left no writings, and only three brief letters. He was a preacher, his words were meant for those who heard him and no-one bothered to preserve those words. Perhaps this is just as well, because preaching depends so much on the person speaking, and the words when written down often do not convey the particular charism that sets them alight.

We have the accounts of those who knew him when they testified at his cause for canonisation, but these are limited and somewhat repetitive, limited as they are by the specific areas set out by the investigating panel. What these testimonies do convey are what could be regarded as ordinary virtues, cheerfulness, compassion, kindness, thoughtfulness for others, all combined in an impressive equilibrium of character, but exhibited in the most trying and heroic of circumstances. There are a few accounts of the miracles he wrought; what is notable about these is how they are always preceded by prayer.

Prayer. This, I feel, leads us to the heart of who Dominic was, a man of prayer. It seems as if he was hidden within the depths of his prayer, even when this prayer was very vocal. It seems to me that we find the key to the true Dominic when we consider those nights of prayer, when he lay before the altar of God, praying, groaning with tears and supplication, not only for the presence of his God, but above all in intercession for the souls he so longed to bring to Christ and for the brothers and sisters in his Order who were spreading the Gospel.

There is his quiet doggedness and refusal to give in to despondency. How many times must he have felt as if his mission was useless and going nowhere after the death of Peter of Castelnau, when the Cistercians returned to their monasteries and he was left almost alone to plough a lonely furrow for those ten years of his life? However, he persevered, rejoicing to share in the sufferings and humiliation thrown at him by the Cathars, seeing such a meagre return for all his work. All that mattered to him was that he was where God wanted him to be and that he was fulfilling the will of God for him at that particular moment.

We can have only an inkling of the charm that won so many over to him as they sensed the presence of God in him, and later caused hundreds of men and women, not only to flock to his sermons, but also to follow him into the Order he had founded. The Dominican Nuns now are also engaged in active work throughout the world.

Gradually, his character revealed itself to me; despite all Dominic's efforts to conceal himself within the blazing light of God, a beautiful personality emerged. He was definitely not the fanatical, bigoted persecutor as some portray him. All his actions show him as one on fire with the love of God, a man of deep, contemplative prayer, a kindly, compassionate man, full of joy and the peace of God.

The Dominican Order

If, especially in the early days of his ministry, his 'successes' were so meagre, this was, perhaps, because his real vocation in life was to found the Order that would continue his work, and be a visible expression of Dominic the Man, when the man Dominic, during his life, was so hidden. The Dominican Order is an embodiment of its Founder and perhaps the height and breadth and depth of his character could find full expression only in his Order and the men and women who joined it. The genius of his preaching was epitomised in Reginald and Jordan, who attracted hundreds to the Order. His openness to the world around him in the light of the Scriptures found full expression in the towering intellects of Albert the Great and Thomas Aquinas. Catherine of Siena knew that she was being faithful to her father in God when she ministered to the sick and suffering, to the criminals and outcasts, and spoke with authority to the Pope himself, for, like Dominic, she had to be wherever the need was greatest.

The Quest for Truth

The motto of the Dominican Order is 'Veritas'—Truth—a concept that throws down a the gauntlet to our age, where the accepted wisdom is a relativism which says that there is no such thing as ultimate truth; a relativism that asserts: 'something is true for you, but that doesn't make it true for anyone else'—especially if it is religious truth. Not so, says Thomas Aquinas, the great Dominican; there is ultimate truth, and if our lives are not ordered to that truth then our lives, and ultimately society, will be disordered because it is not grounded in truth. 'Truth must consequently be the ultimate end of the whole universe . . . for the first author and mover of the universe is an intellect . . . and the ultimate end of the universe must, therefore, be the good of an intellect. This good is truth.' The Dominican Order stands as a testimony to this. It has received the office of Preacher and must boldly proclaim the Truth which is Jesus Christ.

The New Gnosticism

Such a form of belief that Dominic met in his day as Catharism bears many resemblances to what Pope John Paul 11 called 'the culture of death' in our own days, a movement that, like Catharism, downgrades marriage, advocates euthanasia and the hatred of new birth in the forms of contraception and abortion. It is no wonder then, that Cathar, Gnostic, beliefs are met with such sympathy among those who in our day hate religion, especially as proclaimed in the Catholic Church, and who prefer the myths of *The Da Vinci Code*. Dominic countered the Cathar heresy by pondering deeply on the Scriptures, and by living in close union with Life Itself in the person of Jesus Christ. He showed by his own way of life the winsomeness, the joy and the attraction of a life lived to the full because lived in God, in other words, in living out of the Gospel of Life. By his own grounding in the Scriptures, aligned with the medieval university disciplines of the secular sciences of his day, he was able to give a reasoned and persuasive alternative to Cathar teachings.

Opposition to the Faith

Dominic was confronted with many of the challenges that the Church faces today: a resurgent Islam, a resolute opposition to the Church, in our days by atheism and secular humanism. Not only in the Islamic world, and in the countries where atheism is the official creed, and elsewhere, Christians – and other faiths – are often under severe persecution; more people are being killed now for their Christian faith than in all the eras that have gone before. In the West, we may not yet be undergoing physical persecution but in many ways the threat is perhaps even more pernicious because it is so underhand. Under the banner of multi-culturism, tolerance, human rights and freedoms, Christians are being discriminated against, sacked from their jobs, brought to court, with laws being passed that deny and legislate against the Christian morals and beliefs that have sustained the West for two thousand years. Dominic, too, had to face opposition and challenge to his faith, and met it with discussion, a deep knowledge of his own faith as well as the beliefs that challenged that faith, so that he could respond rationally and with the burning love of Christ that shone from him.

The Catholic Faith provides a 'sign of contradiction' to the beliefs of the secular world and to other faiths, while acknowledging whatever is good, true and beautiful, and therefore of God, in other faiths. Dominic reminds us that we need to be truly grounded in that faith so that we can respond when challenged, but always 'speaking the truth in love' as he did. He told his novices and his brothers to study always, because we can never come the end of what our faith reveals; every day we can discover new depths. Saint John of the Cross said that we have an infinite capacity for God, because God himself is infinite, and he will always be hollowing out new capacities within us so that we can continually receive more of what He wills to give us.

Faith and Reason

With atheistic rhetoric loudly proclaiming that religion is simply superstition and opposed to reason, we need to look at the example of the medieval universities and the Dominican contribution, to reaffirm the rigour of their training and their understanding that faith and reason are, as Pope John Paul 11 expressed it, the two wings 'on which the human spirit rises to the contemplation of truth'; they are in no way opposed to each other. Indeed, the medieval harmony between faith and reason, and the belief that our universe and our world can be explored and understood because it obeys the laws of a rational God, paved the way, not only for the beginnings of scientific discovery at the time but also for future scientific development. Pope John Paul 11 made the observation that 'From the late Medieval period onwards, however, the legitimate distinction between the two forms of learning became more and more a fateful separation',[14] and this separation has now become rejection and opposition by so many in the scientific world of any other form of philosophy than that of scientific 'realism'. We need to reaffirm these two wings boldly.

---

[14] Faith and Reason 45

Sadly, in today's world those who oppose the faith seem to have such a poor understanding of it that it is difficult to have a genuine discussion with them. So often straw men are put up to represent the faith to be demolished, rather than a genuine grasp of the faith by those who oppose it. With Dominic's example to guide us, we must continually endeavour to put the truth of the Catholic Faith forward in whatever way possible, and challenge the atheistic elite to respond to that, rather than to shadows and distortions of it.

Pope John Paul added that 'God has placed in the human heart a desire to know the truth—in a word, to know himself—so that, by knowing and loving God, men and women may also come to the fullness of truth about themselves'.[15] This observation makes several important points: God has placed in our hearts a hunger for truth, and if we go after lies then our hearts are distorted and left empty. Jesus declared himself to be the truth, so that a denial of Jesus—of the good, the true and the beautiful—is a denial of truth. And if we deny the truth then we do not know ourselves and we fail to grow to the full stature of our humanity that God has willed individually for each one of us, a stature that is the stature of Christ himself.

John Paul 11 also points to why Dominic was so successful in integrating his prayer and study in his discussion of Saint Anselm.[16] 'Saint Anselm underscores the fact that the intellect must seek that which it loves; the more it loves, the more it desires to know. Whoever lives for the truth is reaching for a form of knowledge which

---

[15] Ibid, Introduction
[16] Faith and Reason 42

is fired more and more with love of what it knows, while having to admit that it has not yet attained what it desires.'

Dominic's example encourages us to follow in his footsteps, to be filled with the love of God revealed in Jesus Christ; to seek to know him in ever greater depth, confident in the knowledge that all true searching, within the depths of the deposit of our Faith and in the world around us, can only bring us closer to God who is ever beyond our understanding, but who at the same time encourages us to explore the world He has made, and to ever greater knowledge of Himself.

BIBLIOGRAPHY

Balthasar, Hans Urs von	The Scandal of the Incarnation Ignatius Press 1990
Bedouelle, Guy O.P.	Saint Dominic, the Grace of the Word Ignatius Press 1987
Cahill, Barbara O.P.	Dominic the Preacher DLT 1988
Churton, Tobias	The Gnostics Weidenfeld & Nicolson 1987
Dorcy, Sister Mary Jean O.P.	Saint Dominic Tan Books 1959
Green, Michael	The Books the Church Suppressed, Monarch Books 2005
John Paul 11, Pope	Encyclical, Faith and Reason
Koudelka, Vladimir	Dominic DLT 1997
Lehner Francis O.P.(Ed)	Saint Dominic, Biographical Documents Thomist Press 1964
Oldenbourg, Zoe	Massacre at Monségur Phoenix Press 1961
Pernoud, Regine	Those Terrible Middle Ages Ignatius Press 2000
Simon, Bernard	The Essence of the Gnostics Arcturus Press 2004
Tugwell Simon O.P. (Ed.)	Early Dominicans SPCK 1982
Vann, Gerald O.P.	To Heaven with Diana! Collins 1960